Paid in Karma 2

Lock Down Publications and Ca$h
Presents
Paid in Karma 2
A Novel by *Meesha*

Paid in Karma 2

Lock Down Publications
P.O. Box 870494
Mesquite, Tx 75187

Visit our website @
www.lockdownpublications.com

Copyright 2020 by Meesha
Paid in Karma 2

Lock Down Publications
Like our page on Facebook: Lock Down Publications @
www.facebook.com/lockdownpublications.ldp
Cover design and layout by: **Dynasty Cover Me**
Book interior design by: **Shawn Walker**
Edited by: **Jill Duska**

Stay Connected with Us!

Text **LOCKDOWN** to 22828 to stay up-to-date with new releases, sneak peaks, contests and more…

Thank you.

Submission Guideline.

Submit the first three chapters of your completed manuscript to ldpsubmissions@gmail.com, subject line: Your book's title. The manuscript must be in a .doc file and sent as an attachment. Document should be in Times New Roman, double spaced and in size 12 font. Also, provide your synopsis and full contact information. If sending multiple submissions, they must each be in a separate email.

Have a story but no way to send it electronically? You can still submit to LDP/Ca$h Presents. Send in the first three chapters, written or typed, of your completed manuscript to:

LDP: Submissions Dept
Po Box 870494
Mesquite, Tx 75187

DO NOT send original manuscript. Must be a duplicate.

Provide your synopsis and a cover letter containing your full contact information.

Thanks for considering LDP and Ca$h Presents.

Chapter 1
Justice

"Justice! Justice, wait!" Wes called out as I ran fast as I could to get out of the room.

Anger, disgust, anxiety, horror, pain, embarrassment, and disappointment were only some of the emotions I felt as I fled onto the street. The image of Shanell bouncing on my husband's dick kept flashing before my eyes and the sounds of them fucking rang in my ears repeatedly. There was no way to make any of it go away.

Tears fell from my eyes as I ran top speed down the street. As I turned the corner, I tripped over the curb and fell on my knees. The ache in my legs was nothing compared to the pain I felt in my chest. As I let out a gut-wrenching howl, a woman rushed to my aid.

"Oh my God, are you alright, baby?" she asked in a shaky voice. "Should I call 911?"

Glancing up at her, all I could do was shake my head no. How could I explain to a complete stranger that my husband had deceived me in the worst way? Thinking about everything Shanell had done dried my tears instantly. The hurt turned to anger and my heart turned cold.

"I got her," Dap said, trying to lift me from the ground by my arms.

"Don't touch me, Dap!" The woman stepped closer to me with her phone in her hand.

"I said I got her! You can take yo' ass on somewhere, Susan. She's not in any type of danger," Dap growled, causing the woman to scurry away.

"You knew!" I screamed, pushing him away. "When you told Tana that Wes was home sleeping, you failed to mention the same bitch that has been trying to destroy our lives was laying with him!" Climbing to my feet, I stared him in the face, but couldn't read his expression.

"You helped him cover up his deception, but it came back full force, biting him in the ass! Tell your brother I tried to see things from his perspective, but I won't sit around and watch him disrespect me. If Shanell is who he wants, she can have his slimy ass!"

"Justice, it's not what you think. Seeing the shit with your own eyes is hard, I know. But that video is a lie. Trust me."

"How the fuck can you tell me what I saw was basically a delusion? My husband was fucking for all to see, Dap! I won't let you stand here and make me out to be the crazy one! Wes fucked up for the last time with me. I'm done!"

"You have to hear him out, Justice! Shit is bad, really bad, but he is innocent. I'll put my life on the line and stand by it."

"Save it! There's nothing your brother can say to me, Dap. I saw everything I needed to see on that projector back there. That's your brother. You're supposed to have his back through thick and thin. Do me a favor and bring my baby to me so I can leave. I'll take an Uber, because I'm not going back in there."

Leaving him standing in the middle of the sidewalk, I went into the Starbucks and ordered a latte. When I looked out the window, Dap was no longer standing where I had left him. When my name was called, I sat at an empty table and let the tears fall freely. My phone vibrated and I pulled it from my pocket. Tana was calling.

"Tana, bring my baby to the Starbucks around the corner," I said without saying hello.

"Nah, get your ass back over here. Something ain't right with this shit. Wes Sr. ended the shower and put everybody out. There's no one here except family."

"Fuck that family! They're going to side with him anyway!" I cried.

"That's where you're wrong, sis. Beverly is tearing Wes a new asshole as we speak. He said Shanell drugged him, and I believe him. Come back. I'll be waiting for you outside." Tana hung up before I could respond.

Picking up my latte, I left and made my way back to the venue to see what the fuck was really going on.

Chapter 2
Beverly

When the video of Wes and Justice changed from Brian McKnight's *Crazy Love* with pictures of Wes, Justice, and Faith to porn, I was appalled. Wes stood there like a deer caught in headlights. Poor Justice escaped embarrassment by darting out of the building and I didn't blame her. She was better than me though, because I would've been whooping my husband's ass. Everybody's eyes were glued to the screen and that pissed me off even more.

"Turn that shit off now!" I screamed over the moans coming through the speakers.

My brother Steve rushed across the room and pulled the cord from the wall. Once the room was silent, I glanced around, mugging everybody.

"Somebody in this muthafucka has some explaining to do. This was an invite only event and the bitch on that video wasn't invited. If she was here, it's because somebody told her the location to display her bullshit. This is low down, and when I find out who did this, I'm fuckin' them up. Just to let y'all know, the party is over. I'm sorry about everything, but we have to get to the bottom of this situation," I said mainly to Justice's co-workers.

Watching as everyone made their way out of the building, I could see them whispering amongst themselves. I hoped like hell they would forget what they had witnessed and keep it away from folks that weren't present. The last thing Justice needed was returning to work and being the talk of the establishment. The surprise baby shower was ruined, but the surprise was a mystery that needed to be solved. I handed Faith to Tana and stalked over to my son.

"What the fuck were you thinking? Do not try to tell me that was an old video because I know for a fact it's not. That room is in your damn home, Wes! After all that bitch put you through, you're still sleeping with her?"

"Ma, I don't remember none of that shit! The last thing I remember from Friday to Saturday is having drinks with Stew and waking up after Dap threw ice water on me," he explained with tears welling in his eyes. "I swear, I didn't do this, Ma. Shanell drugged me somehow. Dap read the note she left on the bed admitting she did it. I've been drawing a blank trying to figure out how. I never saw her at the bar."

"How did she get back to your house, Wes?" I asked.

"I don't know!" he yelled. "I wouldn't go back to Shanell after what she has done. She set me up! Justice is not going to believe any of what I'm saying, but it's the truth."

"Lower your voice when you're addressing my wife," my husband said, stepping in Wes' face. "You did this shit to yourself. If Shanell drugged you, we need to get you to the hospital to see if there are any traces of it in your system. If it is, her ass is getting locked the fuck up this time. Now we need to figure out how the fuck that video got *here*."

"Where is Justice?" one of her cousins asked.

"Conya, she's outside. Come with me, you and Keianya," Tana said, handing Faith back to me. "Beverly, I'll be right back."

I loved Tana because she was like me in so many ways and was down for whatever. My eyes fell on Bria and she was sitting at an empty table, tapping away on her phone. Wes Sr. followed the direction I was staring and the frown on his face deepened.

"Bria, was Shanell in this building?" His voice boomed through the room. Bria looked up without a care in the world and rolled her eyes before going back to whatever she was doing on her phone. "Do you hear me taking to you, Bria? If I have to walk over there, you're not going to like the outcome."

"Why would Shanell be here? That would be stupid," she said smartly.

"Do you know anything about that video mysteriously appearing on that projector?" I asked. When she purposely ignored me talking to her, I looked at my husband. "Baby, would you hold Faith? Never mind. Wes, get your baby. I have to take care of something."

Wes grabbed the baby from my arms and I wasted no time storming in my daughter's direction. She placed her phone on the table and stood up quickly. Bria's attitude had been shitty towards me for quite some time and she felt she didn't have to talk to me unless she wanted to. Usually I'd let her have that shit, but not today. I felt she knew more than she was letting on, but I was going to let her hang herself with this one.

"I'm going to ask you again. Do you know anything about the video?" Bria still refused to answer the question, so I asked another one to see if she would respond or stay silent. "Have you spoken to Shanell since you've been back home?"

"You don't care about Shanell. Why are you worried if I've talked to her or not?" she shot back.

"That's correct, I don't care for her, but you did witness what happened along with the rest of us. What do you know about the video, Bria? It didn't appear here by itself. How did it make its way into this building?" I sneered, getting in her face. "The wheels are turning in my head and you are the only person who has access to Shanell. Did you put the video out so Justice could see it for Shanell?" My patience was wearing thin and Bria was seconds away from getting beat the fuck up.

"First of all, I'm not the only one that's still in contact with Shanell. Your son is obviously still bumping pelvises with her and sharing bodily secretions," she smirked. "Secondly, it was time to prove Wes wasn't shit. He's your favorite anyway. But who's gonna check me about it?" she asked, folding her arms over chest as she cut her eyes at me.

Wes Sr. rushed over to where we were and stood by my side. "Bria, are you saying you were the one that put that video on the projector?"

"I did it. Shanell didn't deserve what Wes did to her. The way he left her out in the cold was wrong and he deserves everything she's doing to him. I guess the next question is going to be, why am I helping her, huh?"

"Bria, I've been there for you through everything and you stab me in the back for a vindictive bitch?" Wes yelled as he walked across the room. "I'm your fuckin' brother, man! This bitch could've harmed my fuckin' daughter and you wouldn't even tell me where to find her! Fuck everything else she did. Faith didn't have shit to do with any of this!"

"Faith is the name you and Shanell picked out for the daughter y'all was having together! Nigga, you ain't shit giving the name to a baby you had with another woman. How do you think that made her feel when she found out about it? She was ready to kill herself, Wes! You left her knowing she has mental problems and you didn't give a fuck as long as you had your precious wife."

"Damn right, bitch. I'm who he's supposed to give a fuck about." Justice came out of nowhere, walking toward Bria. "You got your muthafuckin' nerve standing there defending a bitch who would probably turn on your ass if given the chance! Since you want to be her spokesperson and act on her behalf, you can take this ass whoopin' that's meant for her too."

Before anyone realized what was happening, Justice charged Bria and punched her in the mouth. Bria fell back on the table and Justice pounced on her, pummeling her face with her fist. It took Wes Sr., Donovan, and Justice's uncle Jesse to get Justice off Bria.

"Justice, let her go!" my husband yelled, prying her hand out of Bria's hair. "That's enough!"

When Bria and Justice were finally separated, Bria charged toward Justice and was snatched back by Donovan. She jerked away from him and tried to go after Justice again.

"Bria, I said cut the shit out!" he said, gripping her arm tightly.

"I bet yo' ass won't try to fight that hoe's battles no more. Tell her she's next, because I got a size eight and a half that I want to put up her ass," Justice said, laughing. "Y'all gon' learn that even though I'm quiet and look passive, I'm just as crazy as that looney bitch. I don't know what type of females y'all had to fight off behind Wes, but I'm not one of them. Justice Page-King is cut from a different cloth, baby."

"Tana, take her outside," Donovan said while still holding Bria.

"I'm not going nowhere! I want to know, what did she have to gain from pulling this stunt? It's more to the story that she ain't telling and I want to hear it."

"Bitch, you wouldn't be able to handle the muthafuckin' truth! You better shut the fuck up while you have a chance. Save face and take your ass on somewhere," Bria snapped.

"Jesse," Wes Sr. called out to Justice's uncle and then he nodded his head toward the door. "Take Tana and your daughters, because they looking like they ready too."

Jesse looked at Justice sternly as she walked toward the exit. She suddenly came back and walked up to Wes and took Faith out of his arms. "I'm leaving. Don't expect me to be at the house," she said, walking away without looking back.

Wes started to follow Justice and Tana shook her head slowly. "This is not the time, Wes. Nine times out of ten, Justice and the baby will be at my house. Give her a minute, because this is another blow on y'all marriage. Figure this shit out and contact her tomorrow or something. I want you to know, I'm fuckin' your sister up."

"I'm standing right here! You don't know shit about me, bitch!" Bria screamed.

"And you don't know nothing about me either, but you gon' remember this ass whopping that I'm about to dish out though," Tana said, walking in Bria's direction.

"Tana, bring yo' ass on here," Jesse snarled, grabbing the back of her shirt.

"Yeah, take that bitch on!" Bria laughed, running her hand through her hair.

"Bria, what is your problem? I've never seen you act like this before," my husband snapped.

"I don't have a problem, and I've never known you to lie to me either, but I guess we've both seen another side of each other, huh?" she shot back.

"Bria, if you have something you want to get off your chest, now is the time to do it," I said, shooting daggers in her direction. "You've had your ass on your shoulders for quite some time, and I want to know why."

The room got utterly quiet waiting for whatever Bria had to say. The expression on Wes's face frightened me a bit because it seemed like he wanted to attack his own sister. Bria was the only person

13

who seemed to be unbothered about the entire situation. Her only concern was her hair being out of place.

"All my life I've come third in y'all life when it came to Wes. Hell, Donovan too, if you want me to be truthful. I've always felt like an outcast when it came to you, *Mom*."

"That's not true, Bria. We loved all of y'all equally. We may have been a little strict with you because you were the baby girl of the family, but the love was the same," Wes Sr. replied to what she said. "What you did here today has nothing to do with you not getting the love you felt you deserved."

"It has everything to do with it! Wes could do no wrong, and I had to show y'all that he wasn't the perfect son y'all made him out to be. When he went to prison, he was y'all main concern. I was put on the back burner. It was all about Wes! I was even dealing with his bullshit while he was away. Shanell was going through so much and he wasn't there!" Bria screeched.

"Shanell didn't let any of us know what was going on with her, and neither did you!" I retorted. "For you to say you were pushed to the side, that's a lie. We've always had your front and your back, Bria!"

"Nah, my daddy always had my back, *Beverly*. You never loved me!"

"Bria, what the hell has gotten into you?" my husband asked.

"I've been holding shit in for years, and the two of y'all never even considered telling me the truth!" she said, looking back and forth between my husband and me. "Don't act like neither one of you are clueless of what I'm talking about either."

"I have no clue what you're talking about. How about you tell us," I said, walking slowly toward her with my hands outstretched. "Tell me what's going on, baby?" Bria stood openly crying and I gathered her in my arms, but she stepped away from me.

"Did it ever occur to any of y'all why I left Chicago?" she asked. Not waiting for an answer, she continued. "Well, let me tell you what I found out five years ago. When the two of you went on vacation to Columbia, I lost my Social Security card and knew there was a duplicate in your closet," she said, looking at me.

"I went in your closet to search for it because I had just got a job and needed it. While sifting through the file cabinet in your closet, I came across some old letters that were addressed to you, Dad. Do you know who those letters were from?" Bria asked, turning to him with tears streaming down her face.

"Your mother," he whispered.

"My what? I didn't hear you!" she yelled.

"I said your mother."

Wes and Donovan had shocked expressions on their faces. My head fell down until my chin landed on my chest. I felt my own tears gliding down my cheeks. Now I knew why Bria tried her best to stay away from me all these years.

Chapter 3
Bria

Beverly's demeanor told me she knew exactly where I was going with my rant. Focusing on my father, he kept opening and closing his mouth, but no words came out. All of a sudden, the tables turned and I had the upper hand on all them muthafuckas.

"What is she talking about, Pop?" Wes's stupid ass asked. Bubba from the movie *Forest Gump* could've picked up on what I said.

"She's implying that Beverly's not her mother. Is that what you're trying to say, Bria?" Dap asked.

"I'm not trying to say shit! Your father already confirmed it. She's not my mama! I want to know why I am twenty-five years old and wasn't told!"

"Bria, watch your mouth," my father said calmly. "I didn't know how to tell you. Beverly has been your mother since you came home from the hospital when you were two months old." I loved my father, but he was crazy as fuck if he thought I was about to shrivel because he was glaring at me.

"That woman has never been a mother to me! It has always been about Wes and Donovan. The sad part about all of this is the fact Donovan isn't even her biological son, but nobody knew until it was told. I've noticed how you looked at me with disgust, but it was done quickly. I didn't realize why until the pieces started falling in place. Everything was always my fault when things went wrong and I didn't do anything most of the time. Daddy, most of the things I wanted came from you, not Beverly,"

"Bria, I've never mistreated you. We did things together all the time and you were always happy. I understand now why you distance yourself from me. This is the reason I get nothing but attitude from you whenever I call to check on you. Why didn't you come talk to me about what was on your mind?"

"It wasn't my job to come to you! Who's the parent? You chose to play mama to a child that you passed off as your own. Y'all should've been running off at the mouth once I was old enough to understand what was going on. But that was too hard of a task for either of you to do. Why wasn't I told the truth!?

"Beverly, don't answer that. Bria, we will talk about this later at the house. This is not the time nor the place for this discussion," my father stated.

"There's nothing to discuss. You know now that I helped Shanell get back at Wes and exposed his ass, and I finally let it be known that I knew about my fake-ass life for years. I have one more thing to say before I head out." I smirked, walking backwards toward the rear exit. "Shanell isn't finished with you, brother. Don't ask me shit about it because I don't know shit. Fuck y'all!" Holding my middle fingers up on both hands, I laughed all the way out the door.

"Bria! Bria, come yo' ass back here!"

My father's voice followed me until the door closed. Sticking the two by four under the handle of the door so it couldn't be opened from the inside, I jumped in my car and drove the fuck off.

The moment I had pressed play for the video to play on the projector, I pulled my phone out to change my flight. Staying in Chicago was something I had no plans of doing. If my father wanted to talk, he would have to come see me on my turf. As I drove to my destination, my phone was blowing up. I didn't bother to check it because I knew it was one or all of my family members on the other end.

Instead, I declined the next call and dialed a number of my own. The phone rang and went to voicemail after a while. Redialing the number, I prayed the call would be answered the second time around.

"Hello."

"Sage, where is Auntie Nell?" I asked, wondering why my son was answering Shanell's phone.

"She's hiding, Mommy. We playing hide go seek and Auntie is hiding real good. I been looking for her a long time too," Sage said sadly.

"Baby, call out to Auntie and tell her Mommy is on the phone," I told him in a shaky voice.

"Auntie, Mommy is on the phone!" he screamed loudly. "She said come out and get the phone!"

My heart was thumping in my chest because Shanell's apartment wasn't that big. Something had to be wrong because she should've been to the phone by now. I started feeling lightheaded and had to remind myself to breathe. Lowering the window to let some cool air inside the car, I listened as Sage continuously called out to Shanell.

Pressing down on the gas pedal, I dodged through traffic until I got to the expressway. It would take me fifteen minutes tops to get to Shanell's apartment, and I was about to make it there in a little over five. I connected my phone to the Bluetooth so my hands were free.

"Sage, go sit on the couch and turn on the cartoons. Mommy will be there soon, but don't hang up the phone. I will talk to you until I get to the door, okay?"

"Okay, Mommy. Hurry because I'm a big boy, but not big enough to be in Auntie's house by myself. What if the police come and take me like they did those kids on the news? Remember you told me they took the kids because they stupid mama left in the house by they self?"

"Sage, the police are not going to take you anywhere. I promise. Mommy will be there before anybody even notices you're there alone. Did you find the cartoons on the TV?" I asked, trying my best not to let him know I was scared.

"Yes, *SpongeBob* is on, Mama, and the TV ain't too loud. Just like you taught me," he said happily.

"Good, baby. Did you eat?"

"Yes, I had a peanut butter and jelly sandwich with a cold glass of milk. You know that's my favorite, silly."

"I know, baby," I said, dodging cars without causing an accident.

Shanell had some explaining to do because she knew better than to leave Sage alone in an apartment by himself. Anything could've happened to him. Signaling to get off the expressway at 79th Street, I zoomed up the ramp and made the right at the light. Traffic was heavy on 79th so I made a right on Michigan and shot fast as I could to 81st Street. Going east on the street, I took it all the way to Eberhart Avenue. Making a left, I drove to 80th and was lucky enough to find a park a few buildings away from Shanell's.

I grabbed my phone and purse and damn near ran into the building. "Sage, open the door for Mommy," I said into the phone as I knocked.

"Okay, I'm coming." Sage fumbled with the lock, but he finally got it open.

Twisting the knob, I pushed the door open and my baby fell into my arms hugging me tightly.

"Mommy!" Sage screamed happily, throwing his arms around my neck tightly. "I'm glad you came for me."

"I'll always protect you, baby," I said, prying him off me.

Closing the door, I led Sage back to the couch so he could finish watching cartoons. I was fuming inside because Shanell was dead wrong leaving him alone in her apartment. The fact that I couldn't call her pissed me off even more because she had left her phone with Sage.

Over an hour had passed and Shanell hadn't come back in the house. Sage was lying across my lap while I checked the many emails I had from clients when I heard a set of keys outside the door. "Go into the back room, baby. I have to talk to Auntie for a minute, then we are leaving."

Sage got up from the couch and did what I asked. Surprisingly, he walked instead of running like he usually did. Shanell opened the door with a smile on her face but when she saw me, it dropped like a bad habit.

"I wasn't expecting you back until later. How long have you been here?" she asked nonchalantly.

"Long enough to know my son was here alone. What the fuck were you thinking, Shanell?" I asked, standing from the couch.

"Girl, bye. Wasn't nothing going to happen to him. Sage is a man trapped in a little boy's body. You may as well call him Charles Lee Ray Jr. He was cool, Bria. What you mad for?" she had the nerve to ask, going into the kitchen.

"Shanell, Sage is five! Anything could've happened to him. You don't leave a child unsupervised at any given time!"

"My mama left me alone all the time. I didn't die and I came out fine, as you can see," she smirked.

"You are far from fine, Shanell. You're off your meds and making irrational decisions. The shit was irresponsible on your part. Don't worry, I'm glad you're back because Sage and I are about to head to the hotel and then to the airport. I'm going home tonight."

"Bria, you have to tell me what happened at the shower, girl," Shanell said excitedly, coming back into the living room. "Did you play the video?"

I sighed loudly. I wasn't in the mood to relive the incident of the baby shower. All I wanted to do was go home and live my life with my son. "Shanell, I played the video and Wes's deception was out for all to see. That was the last time I'll be in the middle of the bullshit between you and my brother. When you call, please don't discuss Wes at all. I no longer want to be part of your revenge. To be honest, I think you should just leave them alone and move on with your life. Let it go, sis."

"Let it go? You got to be kidding me, right? I'm not letting shit go and you've been involved in all of this from the beginning, so there's no getting out. When your part of the equation gets out for all to see, your family will want nothing to do with you when they find out how deep you are in all of this," she smirked. "You don't want to fuck with me, Bria."

"You can't threaten me with the bullshit, Shanell. There's nothing you can say to my family that I'm worried about because they are already mad at me for showing the video. I really don't give a fuck. Come on, Sage, we're about to go," I yelled.

Shanell approached me quickly, grabbing my throat tightly. "I will bury your ass, bitch! You will do whatever the fuck I tell you to do, so be ready when I call your stupid ass. Stop playing with me, because you know I'm not wrapped tight and I give no fucks for anybody but myself. At this point it's me against the world. Yo' ass is just my pawn until I holla checkmate."

She was foaming at the mouth and her grip got tighter with every word she spoke. I regretted going against my brother now that I knew how unstable Shanell really was. All I wanted to do was get far away from Chicago without any intentions of looking back.

"I got my jacket, Mommy. I'm ready," Sage said, running from the room.

Shanell let my go of my throat before Sage could see what was going on, glaring in my direction. "Safe travels, sis. Call me when you get home. And I mean that shit, call me when you get home," she said, turning to Sage. "You be good, nephew, and remember, TeeTee loves you." She bent down and kissed him on the cheek.

I made sure Sage had his jacket zipped and walked over to the couch, snatching my purse and phone from the table. Without saying goodbye, I took his hand and left the apartment, thinking of ways to get out of the predicament I'd gotten myself into with Shanell.

Chapter 4
Justice

"Justice, why did you do that girl like that?" my uncle Jesse asked as he escorted us out of the building.

"Did you not see what she put on display for everybody to see? Then on top of that, she basically bragged about being the one that did it and all because she's jealous of her brother! Bria is helping the bitch that has been trying to turn our lives upside down and I was supposed to let that shit fly? Not on my watch."

"All I'm saying is, you've come a long way from the girl you used to be. This broad Shanell is not worth you turning back the hands of time. Remember, I was there during the days of you getting locked up for fighting. Justice, you are a grown woman, a mother now, and you won't get locked up with a slap on the wrist this go 'round. They will lock your ass up and throw away the key."

"I don't care about going to jail when it has something to do with my family. My mama protected me at all costs, and I plan to do the same for Faith. If that means going to jail, I'm all for it. What I won't do is walk around watching my back to see which direction a bitch coming for me next."

Jesse shook his head and walked toward his car before turning back around. "When you find yourself in hot water, I'm a phone call away. You weren't wrong for beating that girl's ass back there, but you can't let anybody get to you like that. Play it smart, Justice," he said.

"Daddy, you know we ain't letting this shit ride," Keianya snapped. "I'm pissed because I had to learn about all the drama today," she said, cutting her eyes at me. "Justice isn't the only one this bitch has to worry about now."

"Y'all will be sitting locked together, because I'm not bailing all y'all out."

Uncle Jesse walked to his car and wasted no time pulling out of the parking lot, leaving us standing there watching him merge into traffic. All I could think about was the video that played on the projector. On the inside I wanted to break down and cry a river, but on the outside, I tried my best to hide the hurt that was tearing me apart.

My façade was not flying by Tana because she knew me better than I knew myself. My cousins, on the other hand, only knew what I wanted them to know. We all grew up together, but when I changed my ways, Tana was the only one that followed the path along with me. Conya and Kei, as we called Keianya, were the epitome of ghetto.

"Since his ass is gone, let's go back in there and whoop that trick," Kei said heatedly. "The shit she pulled was foul. I need to hear everything from the beginning, but after we kick her ass again."

"I'm done with that shit, Cuz. I just want to go home," I said. "Who is dropping us off?"

"I'll take you home, but I still want to handle what's inside that building!" Kei yelled.

"Girl, shut yo' ass up!" Conya snapped. "Justice wants to leave it alone and that's what we'll do for now. I'm with Kei though, we need to know what's going on because we are in the dark."

"We can talk about it on the way. Let's just get away from here," I said, walking to Kei's car.

Faith had fallen asleep and I was glad because her diaper bag was in Wes's car along with her car seat, but I didn't care about any of that. Kei unlocked the doors and I hopped in the backseat while Conya got in the front. Tana climbed into the car on the other side and sat beside me. As Kei drove out of the parking lot, the inside of the car was quiet until Conya broke the silence.

"What happened, Justice?"

By the time we made it to my house, the story was out in the open to my cousins and they were ready to set shit off like Queen Latifah and the crew. One thing I can say is both of them had me laughing at a fucked situation. I missed my cousins and I kind of hated the fact of not staying in contact with them.

We all piled out of the car and I switched Faith to my other arm so I could get my keys out of my pocket. Unlocking the door, I punched the code into the alarm pad before I headed upstairs.

"Wait for me in the living room. I have to get Faith cleaned up," I said over my shoulder.

Lying Faith on the changing table, I removed her clothes and gathered a Pamper and baby wipes to dry her butt that was soaking wet. Movement behind me caused me to turn my head slightly to see who was there.

"Are you okay, sis?" Tana asked, standing beside me.

"I'll be alright, Tana. I'm not going to let this break me," I said, wiping Faith down. "I've done everything to prove I'm all for Wes and he keeps fuckin' up. Going back and forth between me and Shanell is not going to work for me. I'm leaving, and he can deal with the craziness that involves her."

"Justice, I told you that I believe Wes when he said he was drugged. I saw his face on the video and I think you should hear him out. I texted Donovan and told him to make sure he got the device the video was downloaded on. You may not want to, but I think you should look at that video in its entirety."

"I'm not watching my husband have sex with another female! Are you out of your mind?" I snapped.

"You have to, because leaving your marriage without hearing all the details would be a mistake. Justice, I'm all for you leaving this marriage if your husband is on bullshit, but I don't believe that's the case here. She did something to him, and it's in that video."

I wasn't trying to hear shit Tana was saying because my mind was already made up. I saw what I saw and that was that. There was nothing anyone could say or do to tell me different. The bottom line was, my husband stuck his dick in another woman's twat and it was recorded and brought to my attention. How he ended up in the predicament was on him because I was out of town when everything went down. To make matters worse, the shit happened in my home. He could've at least taken the bitch to a damn hotel or the Motel 6.

"Are you listening to me?" Tana asked, cutting into my thoughts.

"You want the truth or a lie? Nah, I wasn't listening because I don't care anymore," I said, fastening the last button on Faith's sleeper. Picking her up, I walked her to the crib and placed her inside. As I made sure the monitor was on, I walked out of the nursery and down the short hall to my bedroom.

"You put Faith to bed, so does that mean you're staying here tonight?"

"Tana, I'm sleeping in the guest room until I can find a place of my own. There's too much shit for me to pack up for the baby alone," I responded, grabbing the hangers that held my clothes. "Help me move my shit please."

I walked down the hall and placed the hangers in the empty closet of the guest room and went back for more. Kei and Conya joined us and we had all of my things moved in no time. There was no conversation because everyone knew, once I said drop a subject, that's what I meant. When the last of my plastic shoe containers was brought in, I was tired as hell.

"We're about to leave, cousin. Maybe we can get together this weekend. Go out to eat or something," Conya said as we headed down the stairs. "But I want you to call us if that bitch gets out of pocket before then. You don't have to fight this shit alone. We got yo' back."

"You got that shit right! I'm ready to put a bitch's head between a rock and a hard place," Kei said as the front door opened and the alarm beeped.

Wes and Dap walked in and I turned around and headed back upstairs. I wasn't in the mood to talk about shit with my dumb-ass husband. "Sounds like a plan. I'll see y'all later."

"Justice, where are you going?" Tana asked.

"Far away from that nigga," I said, walking down the hall to the guest room and slamming and locking the door. Lying on the bed, I covered my eyes with my arm and thought about my next move.

Chapter 5
Wes

The shit Bria pulled had me thirty-eight hot. What she revealed shocked me, but I couldn't overlook the fact that my own sister would stoop so low as to hurt my wife. I understood why she had hatred in her heart for my mother, but what the fuck did that have to do with me? When she learned the truth about her birth mother, she should've talked that shit out with our parents. Instead, she held it in without saying anything about it, then exploded.

When she left the venue after basically saying fuck us, Pops ran out the front, but by the time he got around back, Bria was nowhere to be found. It had been a long time since I'd seen my father hurt to that magnitude. He was cussing and kept calling her phone, but she never answered. We packed up all the gifts and Dap and I left after making sure my parents were good in their car.

On the road to my house, Dap drove in silence while I thought about going to an empty house. Justice made it clear that she wouldn't be there when I arrived.

"Bro, Justice has to watch the video. That's the only way she will believe Shanell drugged you," he said, glancing over at me.

"That shit is going to be awkward as fuck. That's grounds for her to shoot my ass. You must've forgot, my wife owns a gun, muthafucka."

"She's hurt and upset, but I don't think she will hurt you in that way. You have to do whatever is needed to clear yo' name. I'm gon' be honest with you, Shanell is aiming to fuck yo' life completely the fuck up. She doesn't care who is affected since she doesn't have you. We have to find her, and I think I know just who we need to ride down on."

"That bitch don't fuck with nobody, bro. Everybody she knows, knows me, so she would stay far away."

"Curt, nigga! He's still fuckin' with her ass. She needs some-body on her side, and I'm quite sure she found a way to keep him close by. I'll bet money on that shit," he said, pulling into my drive-way. There was an unfamiliar car parked behind Tana's, so bro pulled in behind Justice's car, since mine was in the garage.

"We probably have to search for him too. But we will worry about that after I talk to my wife," I said, getting out of his ride.

We walked up the steps and I unlocked the door and was happy as hell when I saw Justice walking down the stairs with her cousins and Tana. When she laid eyes on me, she turned around and went right back up as she said her goodbyes over her shoulder without acknowledging me. The smile on my face faded instantly and I felt like I lost my best friend.

"What are you going to do to fix this mess?" one of Justice's cousin's asked.

"I'm sorry, I don't think we were formally introduced. What's your name?" I asked, trying my best not to cuss her out.

"I'm Keianya, but everybody calls me Kei. Since we got that out of the way, answer the question, because this shit got my cousin soft as puddin', and that's not how we roll in these streets."

"Any and everything needed, because I'm not gon' lose my wife over bullshit. That video wasn't what it seems, like I said back at the venue," I explained, knowing I didn't have to, but I did.

"From the little bit I saw, it seemed like you were enjoying the hoe riding the fuck outta ya dick," Justice's other cousin snapped. "Before you ask, my name is Conya."

"Well, Conya, did you see me really responding in that clip?"

"I saw your hand on her ass, but the video was cut off before too much could be exposed. My question is, how the fuck did she end up in your crib? According to Miss Beverly, she said that's where the video was made," she asked, folding her arms and rolling her eyes.

"If y'all was listening, I explained the last thing I remember was being at the bar, and I can't recall anything else after that."

"There's a whole muthafuckin' alarm on this crib. Who turned it off so the police wouldn't show up? Inquiring minds want to know, because that shit sounds fishy as hell, Wes," Kei said angrily. "I'm not dumb by a long shot and your story isn't adding up."

She had a point, and I couldn't answer her question at all. I stood dumbfounded because that was a key point I would've asked if the shoe was on the other foot. The way Justice's cousins were interrogating a nigga was embarrassing as hell because I didn't have a comeback at all.

"Hold the fuck up! I don't know y'all from a can of paint and I respect sis to the fullest, but I'm not about to stand here and listen to y'all convict my brother of the bullshit that slimy bitch did to him." Dap was pissed and jumped in quick to defend me.

"Yeah, what we witnessed on the video wasn't good, but we only seen a snippet of what occurred. I have the muthafuckin' drive and we are going to watch it in its entirety and figure this shit out together, since y'all so concerned. Justice, bring yo' ass down here now!"

Dap walked over to the TV and put the USB drive into the port on the side of the sixty-inch TV. Kei and Conya sat on the couch while we all waited for Justice to come downstairs. I turned to face the stairwell as I heard Justice slowly walking down.

"Dap, why the fuck is you screaming in my house and my baby is sleeping? You must've lost your mind."

"Nah, I did just what the hell I needed to do. We are about to get to the bottom of this bullshit tonight. It may not solve all of our problems, but it's a start. You have every right to be pissed, sis. But I know for a fact when I saw my brother yesterday, he wasn't himself. We have to watch this video, Justice. Think about it; why would Wes willingly record himself having sex with another female knowing he has a wife? That shit don't even sound right."

"Dap, I'm not watching my husband have sex with anybody other than me. If you want to play detective, do that shit with all of them," she said, moving her arm back and forth in front of her.

"Baby, you gotta believe me," I said, walking toward her.

"I don't have to do shit, nigga! None of this shit would be happening had you been truthful from day one. You sure know how to pick 'em, I can say that much," she chuckled.

Without warning, Dap started the video and the smirk fell from my wife's face. She slowly descended the last few steps and stood behind the couch. All of our eyes were glued to the TV. Shanell could be seen walking away from the dresser after making sure the camera was positioned correctly. She slowly took the liberty of removing my clothes because it seemed I wasn't capable of doing so. The only movements I made were opening and closing my mouth.

"Look at that bullshit!" Dap exclaimed, pointing at the TV screen. "He's not even coherent. His eyes haven't opened at all. Shanell definitely slipped you a mickey, brah."

When Shanell lowered my briefs over my hips, my joint sprang out and she dropped to her knees, devouring my shit. My body reacted accordingly and I started moaning like a bitch. I wanted to stop the video and put everybody out, but I had to see what transpired. Plus, it was too late; everybody in the room knew what I was working with already.

"He knew what was going on! The way he's gripping the back of her head and feeding her the dick says a lot," Conya snapped back.

"Peep this though, from a man's perspective, that shit is automatic when a bitch slobbin' on yo' knob. You watching this shit in real time just like the rest of us. That bitch knew what the fuck was going on. Wes didn't." My brother was advocating for me to the fullest, and I appreciated it. If I was there alone, I wouldn't have been able to defend myself at all in a room full of women.

At that point, Shanell had climbed on top of me after swallowing my kids in one gulp. My tool was still standing at attention and the sound of Shanell's gushy was vivid in the video. Her moans rang out the speakers and I couldn't believe I was actually watching the bitch rape me in front of my wife.

"You fucked that bitch raw!" Justice screamed.

"I didn't do shit! What part of I don't remember any of this shit don't you understand? It's right there in your face. I was raped!" I yelled without taking my eyes off the screen.

"Did y'all hear that?" Dap asked, rewinding the video a little bit.

"All I heard was Jus and Wes arguing back and forth," Tana responded.

"Nah, everybody shut up a minute," Dap said, turning the volume up louder.

The room was quiet as we waited for him to press the play button. Dap wasn't watching the TV, but he stood with his hand resting on the wall with his eyes closed. He aimed the remote at the TV and held his head down while we listened for whatever he heard the first time around.

"You being real freaky tonight, Justice. I love that shit." I turned and looked at Justice and her expression was blank.

"Whose dick is this?" Shanell moaned while rocking her hips back and forth.

"It's yours, Justice, baby. It's yours," I replied to Shanell's question.

Her hips paused for a second, then she started bouncing on my stick aggressively. She asked the question again and my response was louder, but remained the same. There was no way what was said could be misconstrued by anyone in the room.

"Case muthafuckin' closed! In my nigga's defense, he thought he was fuckin' his wife! If it was anything but, he would've called out that hoe's name, but he didn't. Justice, if you allow that bitch to break up your family, in my eyes, you want to leave anyway. While Shanell thought she was doing something by revealing this video, she didn't do nothing but prove she did something to my brother to put him in this position."

Dap was mad as hell and he stressed a valid point. "She's doing whatever it takes to break up this union, sis. The proof is right here," he said, motioning toward the screen.

Standing to my feet, I rounded the couch until I stood in front of my wife. Grabbing both of her hands, I brought them to my lips and kissed the backs of them. "Baby, I'm sorry for everything and I'm going to make it right. I love you and would never do anything to jeopardize what we have. I don't know what Shanell will try to do after this, but I need you to trust me. You are who I want, not her. We have to deal with this as a family because with us apart, it's not going to work. Are you with me?" I asked, wrapping my arms around her body.

"I'm with you," she said, burying her face in my chest. The tears that flowed from her eyes soaked the front of my shirt, really hurt my heart.

"You better not give in to his ass that fast, Justice," Conya sneered.

"Conya, stay out of their business," Tana cut in. "Whatever the hell she wants to do is on her. This is not the time for you to dictate what the fuck she's planning to do for her family. We know the conniving bitch planned the shit that happened. Let her deal with this however she wants."

"That's the problem! Justice is always letting a nigga wiggle their way back in once they fuck up! She needs to stand up for herself and—"

"Stand up for myself? I've stood up for myself and you whenever the fuck you went through anything! Stop trying to act like I'm a weak-ass bitch, because I've never been that type of woman. This isn't just a relationship. Wes is my muthafuckin' husband, in case you've forgotten. The video opened my eyes to a lot of shit and yes, I believe him. Thank you for bringing me home, but I think it's time for you to leave. We aren't teenagers anymore, Conya. I make my own decisions in this marriage."

"Don't call me when he continues to cheat with this woman that he was enjoying having sex with."

"Conya, you're wrong," Kei said. "Let's go. Justice, I apologize for my sister's actions."

"You don't have to apologize for her. She's a grown-ass woman and meant everything she said." Justice glared at Conya. "To set the record straight, I didn't call on you today. Honestly, I don't know how you ended up at the baby shower in the first place. You and I both know you will call me before I ever call you for anything. I've never needed you, or anyone for that matter. Everybody knows Justice stands strong alone. Get the fuck outta my house!"

Kei pulled Conya by the sleeve of her shirt and led her to the door. Conya turned around abruptly and laughed. "He's going to do you dirty just like the last nigga you thought was going to be there forever. Remember who was there lending a shoulder to cry on."

"Conya, get out of my house before I sweep your ass across this room. I was eighteen years old when that shit happened. I'm no longer the same woman from that time. Laugh your ass out of here, because obviously the years we've been apart from one another have only made you even more jealous of little ole me. Nothing has changed, I see. You only came around to see if my life was miserable as yours, but it's all good. Now go back to the family and talk about me. Just make sure you tell the whole truth of what's going on. In the meantime, don't come near me ever again."

Kei walked to the door and held it open so Conya could leave before her. She mouthed "I'm sorry" and followed her sister out the door. Justice started pacing back and forth across the floor and the anguish was evident in her demeanor.

"Sis, let that shit go," Tana said, sitting on the couch. "It's obvious Conya is still the same envious bitch she was when we were growing up. You know how we do. Ignore the hell out of all that gibberish she was talking."

"I agree. The last thing you need right now is more bullshit on your plate," Dap added. "Wes, we need to make some moves, but first, we should get these bags and Faith's gifts out of the car."

"Where are y'all going?" Justice asked as Faith's cries bellowed through the monitor.

"We gon' try to find out what happened at the bar," Dap responded. "Shanell isn't about to get away with this one," he said, heading for the door.

Kissing Justice on the cheek, I followed my brother out the door so we could get on the road. It didn't take long to gather everything from our cars, but Dap talked to Tana for a minute before we were able to leave on our mission. Stopping Shanell was on my mind heavily, but I didn't know how to put a stop to her madness.

Chapter 6
Dap

Wes and I talked about the video and everything Shanell had done as a whole while I drove downtown to Mary's. I believed I made a mistake playing the video in front of Justice's people. The way her cousin snapped let me know Conya was deep in her feelings. That was something Justice was going to have to figure out on her own. My main objective was to get my hands on Shanell's ass.

We pulled up to Mary's and I had no intentions of paying to valet my shit. I pulled my whip to the curb and hit the hazards as Wes got out. Opening the glove department, I reached in and grabbed my Glock. It was better to be safe than sorry and I wanted to be ready for whatever. Stepping out of my ride, I closed the door and walked toward the entrance of the bar where Wes was waiting.

"Hey, buddy, you can't park there," the valet attendant yelled loudly, strutting in our direction.

"I can and I will, nigga. Watch my shit, and it better be in the same position when I return. So do your job for the free, playa," I said, adjusting my Glock and stalking toward the entrance.

"I'm telling you now, I'm going to have your car towed, sir."

I doubled back to the attendant and stood over him. "Check this out, if I come out this muthafucka and my car gone, yo' ass better be gone with it. My shit better be right where I parked it when I get back. Call the tow truck and see, nigga."

The attendant scowled at me, but I knew for a fact he heard me loud and clear.

Walking to the door of the bar, Wes stood with his hand on the handle. "Why the fuck you strapped, nigga?"

"At one point you didn't need a reason to be strapped, just like me. But the way shits been going, yo' tool needs to be with you at all times," I smirked. "Turn back the hands of time and think back on the nigga you used to be."

"Oh, don't worry about that, I've been thinking about his ass a lot lately. Shanell has been the only muthafucka to bring that shit out of me. I've tried to leave my past in the past—"

Meesha

"Yo' past is on the verge of fuckin' up your future. Leave that mushy *Days of our Lives* shit on Beverly's TV and change the channel to a *Power* episode, nigga," I said seriously, cutting his ass off rapidly. "Open the fuckin' door. We can't ask questions standing out here."

Wes stared at me, but thought better about saying anything to me and went inside the bar. It wasn't busy since it was a Sunday evening and many of the folks had to work the next day. The bartender eyed us from behind the counter, so I chose him for my first round of questioning. As I made my way to the counter, he greeted me right away.

"How may I help you?" he asked nicely.

"Yeah, I came in Friday during Happy Hour with a friend," Wes said slowly.

"I remember you! Man, you were blasted!" The bartender laughed. "Whatever you had before coming here caught up with you quickly. I only gave you three shots and a Corona. The same for the guy you were with. The lady who helped you was God sent. Without her, we would've had to call the cops to arrest you for the night."

Wes pulled his phone out and showed him a picture of Shanell. "Is this her?" he asked.

"Yes, that's her. She truly helped you, man."

"Did you give her any drinks for me? Was she sitting at the table with my friend and I at any given time?" Wes enquired.

The bartender closed his eyes for a minute then opened them again. "As a matter of fact, she did pay for a round for the two of you. Susan poured up the shots and delivered them to you guys. She took care of the entire transaction because we were packed that day. Did something happen?" the bartender asked nervously.

Without answering his question, I glanced around the bar and asked him one of my own. "Is Susan working today?"

"Yeah, she's on break, probably out back having a cigarette. If something happened, let me know because I would have to report it to my boss."

"No, you don't have anything to worry about. Nothing happened. The woman that rescued me mentioned how Susan aided in

36

helping in my time of need. I wanted to give her a hefty tip for going over and beyond her job description." Wes was quick on his feet with the lie he told. Shit, he had me believing he was there to compensate the bitch too.

"That's nice of you, sir. Go through the entryway that has the exit sign and make a left. You can't miss the door at the end of the hall. Susan should be standing right out there by the ashtray."

"Thank you," Wes said over his shoulder as we made our way to the back to find Susan's ass.

As we rushed down the hall, the exit door opened and a blonde-haired Caucasian woman stepped into the building. When she noticed us, her eyes bulged and she stopped in her tracks. Shifting side to side, she backed up as if she was about to try to make a run for the door.

"Susan?" I called out to her. "Don't try to leave out of that door."

"How do you know my name?" she asked in a shaky voice. "What can I help you with?" She was nervous as hell, and that alone told me whatever happened to Wes, happened right inside the bar and Susan helped carry out the deed.

"Show her the picture, bro," I said, never taking my eyes off Susan.

Wes stepped forward and pushed his phone in her face and Susan's eyes danced back and forth rapidly as she studied the image. Turning her head, she looked up at the ceiling and her mouth was moving fast as hell. If I didn't know any better, the bitch was praying to get out of the shit she got herself involved in.

"Have you seen the woman in the photo before? Preferably last Friday," Wes asked calmly.

"No, no, I've never seen her before," Susan stammered.

"Don't stand in my face and lie, Susan. We already know this person was here Friday and you were the one that dealt with her. So, let's try this again. Have you seen her before?" Wes glared at her evilly.

Susan sighed and her shoulders drooped lowly. "I saw her on Friday, but I swear I don't know who she is. The only interaction I had with her was when she placed a drink order. There's nothing more I can say about the individual you are inquiring about." Susan pushed her way between us.

Wes grabbed her arm tightly and yanked her backwards. "I'm not the one to fuck with right now," he snarled. "Peep this though, keep playing me for a fool and yo' ass gon' get slapped the fuck up! What the fuck did the bitch put in my muthafuckin' drink?"

"I—I—I'm so sorry, sir." Susan broke down crying. "I didn't want to do it, but she threatened to shoot me."

"What exactly did you do, bitch?" I asked, pushing her against the wall by her neck. Susan struggled to respond, so I loosened the grip to give her some breathing room to talk.

"I only delivered the drink to this gentleman—" she croaked out, swallowing loudly. "After she dropped a pill in it."

"That shit could've killed my brother! You don't do shit like that to anybody! I should kill yo' ass," I yelled, hitting her head against the wall.

"I swear she forced me to do it! She held a gun to my stomach and I'm pregnant. I did what was asked out of fear for my life, and I had to protect my unborn child. I was given five hundred dollars, but I haven't spent any of it," she cried, digging in her pants pocket. "You can have it back, because I don't want karma to come back and hunt me," she said, holding the money out for Wes to take. "I'm so sorry."

"Hey! What the fuck is going on here?" a fat bald dude asked, stalking down the hall in our direction.

Wes kept his eye trained on Susan and I kept the dude in my line of sight. "Aye, the police will be coming by to speak with you. Don't disappear," Wes barked.

"Please don't call the police!" she cried. "You don't know how scared I've been. She took a picture of my license and knows where I live. She said if I told anybody what happened, she would kill me."

"Susan, what's going on?" the fat muthafucka asked from behind us.

"Nothing, Barry. I'm just talking to my child's father," she said, lying through her teeth.

"Okay, wrap it up. I need you back up front in the next five to ten minutes."

His stumpy ass kept eyeing me and Wes, but finally left us alone in the hall. Deep down I knew Susan was telling the truth. Shanell was more fucked up than any of us knew. Wes stepped away from Susan and gave her a little bit of room. She looked down at the money in her hand and started speaking.

"Today is my last day of work and I'm leaving the city. That woman is crazy. I'm sorry, but I won't be around to answer any questions. I told you all I knew about that nutcase. There's no way I'll live to have my baby if I stay here."

Hearing Susan's side of what happened made me feel bad about putting my hands on her. Shanell didn't care who she bullied to get what she wanted. She had gone as far as threatening a complete stranger to get close to Wes, and that said a lot about how far she would go to ruin him.

"If you feel safe leaving, do that shit," I said, reaching into my pocket. Counting out all the bills, I shook my head and handed the knot to Susan. "Here's thirty-five hundred dollars. Get out of here. I don't ever want to see your face again, understood?"

"Thank you so much. I really—"

"We out, brah. It's time for us to find this bitch, and I know exactly where to start," I said, cutting Susan off and walking back in the direction we came. There was nothing else I wanted to hear from her whiny ass. The only thing that saved her was the fact she was pregnant. In my mind, I had already killed her and put her body in the dumpster.

***

I was mad as hell about the shit Shanell did to that woman and the fact my brother could've died from whatever she gave him. My first mind was to go find Curt, but I had to know what the fuck she put in that drink. There was no way I could go about my day without knowing. As we exited the bar, the attendant was standing with his arms folded over his chest.

"Thanks for looking after my shit, homie," I said, walking around to the driver side of my ride. "I would tip you, but your attitude was foul as hell. Next time maybe you'll be more kind and remember, the customer is always right, nigga."

Sliding in my whip, I sped down the street until I got to Northwestern Memorial Hospital. I entered the parking garage and after finding a parking spot, I got out of the car. Wes was still sitting in the passenger seat like we hadn't made it to our next destination.

"Get out, nigga!" I said, putting my head back in the car.

"What are we doing at the hospital, brah?" Wes asked, puzzled.

"Wes, Shanell slipped you something that made you miss an entire day of your life. The only thing we know is, you fucked her nasty ass and went to sleep. We need to find out exactly what she gave you. Now, come on."

I slammed the door and walked off from his stupid ass. A few minutes later he was out of the car and we were walking into the emergency room. The lobby was actually empty, and that was unusual for a day in Chicago. I sat in an empty chair while Wes went to the counter to check himself in. It didn't take long for them to take him to the back.

While I waited for Wes to take care of his business, I started thinking about Tana. The conversation we had the night before she and Justice left for Arizona, was one I enjoyed. It had been a while since I'd been interested in any woman since things fell off with Kalene almost a year prior.

Kalene was an aspiring model who I hit it off with my first year in California. Beautiful wasn't even the right word to describe her. She was more of an exotic goddess in my eyes. Kalene's skin was the color of a Hershey's chocolate bar and she stood about 5'10" in heels. Everything was going great for us until one day, Kalene was gone. She had cut off her phone and moved out of her apartment without informing a nigga. The shit had me second guessing myself and wondering what I'd done to make her up and leave the way she did. It hurt to know the three years we spent together meant nothing to her sexy ass, and I went on with my life.

Now there was Tana. She wasn't supermodel beautiful, but she was gorgeous in her own way. She was the complete opposite of Kalene, and I could relate to her on a different level. Tana didn't care about having her makeup done to perfection. She actually wore little to none of the cosmetic concoctions that women used. Natural beauty was sexy as hell to me. I pulled out my phone and sent Tana a text just because.

Me: Hey, Beautiful. How's everything going?

I scrolled through my emails while I waited for Tana to respond and one stood out like a sore thumb. After clicking on the document, my eyes scanned the page rapidly and Rocco's words had me confused as hell. Once I finished reading, I closed out of my email and called my mentor immediately. The phone rang a number of times before it was answered.

"Dap, my man," Rocco greeted me in his thick Italian accent. "You got my message, I presume."

"Yeah, I did. What the hell is going on?" I asked.

"There's so much that has been going on prior to you telling me you were considering leaving California. I didn't want to inform you of my mess because I knew you wouldn't have left. This has nothing to do with you, Donovan, but everything to do with me." Rocco was beating around the bush and the shit wasn't sitting well with me.

"Come on, Rocco. You said a lot without saying nothing at all," I said, standing to my feet so I could go outside to talk in private. "Keep it one hunnid with me, man. Why would anyone be looking for me? I haven't done shit to nobody."

"Donovan, calm down. When I handed my business over to you, I did so because I knew you would do right by it. My family isn't fit to run an ice cream truck. As much as I tried to groom my two sons to take over, they weren't for it, and now there's a problem because I've passed it over to someone that isn't a part of our bloodline."

"What do any of this have to do with me? What we have is le-
gally bonded, Rocco. There's nothing wrong with the business ven-
ture we have going on. Even though you signed everything over to
me, you still get ten percent of the profits."

"No, son, I don't. You have to do better with checking your
accounts. I have never cashed any of the checks you've sent. Money
is something I don't need; you know this already."

What Rocco said shocked me because I hadn't noticed that at
all. I made a mental note to go over my bank statements when I had
the chance.

"Arturro and Luciano are full of greed. They will do whatever
it takes to make our lives miserable. I've told them on countless
occasions the problem is with me, not you. No matter how many
times I've told them, both believe you strong armed me somehow.
Don't worry about anything. I will clear all of this up."

"Rocco, if your sons come to me on bullshit, I won't hesitate to
defend myself in any way possible," I said truthfully.

"It won't come to that at all, Dap. I have everything under control, I just wanted to bring everything to your attention. Keep striv-
ing to succeed in your business. I'll always be here for you."

"Rocco, why do I feel you're not telling me everything?" I
asked.

"I said all you need to know. Believe me when I tell you, everything is alright. I'll talk to you later."

Rocco ended the call, leaving me puzzled because I knew there
was more to the story. After walking back into the waiting room, I
sat down, and my phone chimed with a text message from Tana.
She had texted while I was talking to Rocco and I hadn't realized it
until that moment.

*Tana: Everything is cool. I'm still at the house waiting for you
and Wes to come back. Justice went to bed a little bit ago so me and
Faith are chillin' watching TV. When will y'all be back? I don't
want to leave Justice home alone."*

Me: We are at the hospital. I wanted Wes to have tests done to find out what Shanell put in his drink. He's been in the back for a minute but hopefully it won't be too much longer.

Tana: I can't wait to get my hands on this bitch. I'm fuckin' her up!"

Me: Pipe down Holyfield LOL. Don't stress yourself out. I'll be there to escort you home so don't leave until I get there.

Tana: You ain't the boss of me, Dap! Check yaself, homeboy.

Me: What I tell you about that Dap shit? I ain't trying to be ya boss but I guarantee you'll be calling me daddy. I'm coming through hard to sweep you off ya feet, baby girl.

She didn't respond after my rebuttal which was cool because she knew what was up. I did what I set out to do and that was to put it in the atmosphere that she would be mine.

Wes walked from the back after damn near three hours with a frown on his face and papers in hand.

"What did they say, bro?" I asked, rising from the chair I was sitting in.

"I had to pay a nice lil penny for them to expedite the results. Otherwise, I would've had to wait three days to find out." Wes looked down at the papers he held before telling me what I wanted to know. "Shanell slipped Xanax in my drink, man. There's still a substantial amount in my system and if I was required to take a drug test, I'd fail."

Wes' eyes changed from brown to black in a matter of seconds. That was a clear indication he had transformed into the nigga I remembered from back in the day. Whenever he showed that side of him, havoc was being conducted in the streets. Hopefully that was a sign that we would be putting in work soon.

Chapter 7
Curt

"Just the man I was waiting to see. What's up, Bossman?"

My young nigga Flex was overly excited about seeing me. As I stepped inside, I glanced around to make sure wasn't shit flaky going on. The way these muthafuckas moved around nowadays, I had to make sure I stayed on my toes just in case. There were a few items of clothing lying about the living room, and that alone piqued my curiosity.

"Ain't shit up. Everything good around this muthafucka?" I asked, dapping him up.

"Yeah, I'm just happy you came through early because I got a date with this fine-ass cutie though. Time for me to get my dick wet," he laughed.

"Nigga, I don't want to hear all that shit! What's up with those clothes though? I know they don't belong to you because yo' big ass can't get yo' thighs in them skinny-ass jeans."

"Aw, man, I was gon' holla at you about that. I've been letting T-Bone lay low here for a minute because his ole lady put him out." I shook my head. Flex knew from my silence I was pissed. "Hear me out, Curt. I know you don't want nobody in here—"

"Then why the fuck did you make the decision without consulting with me first?" Without giving him a chance to respond, I went in on his ass. "I want his ass out because if my shit grows hands and walks outta this muthafucka, both of you niggas gon' take ya last breath. Pack his shit up and take it to him. If I come back and he's in here doing anything other than selling a pack, we gon' have a major fuckin' problem. Now go get my money so I can bounce!"

Flex walked to the back bedroom and I took my time surveying my spot. There were dishes piled in the sink, shoes under the table, and a pair of women's underwear by the back door. I got pissed as I strolled back to the living room. Flex came waltzing from the back with a duffle bag slung over his shoulder.

"Aye, you need to clean this muthafucka up before you go anywhere. I'll be back to make sure it's done. If T-Bone in this muthafucka when I return, I'm fuckin' him up, and then I'm coming to yo' crib to beat yo' body. This shit don't make no sense. And keep them hoes outta here! This ain't no fuckin' hotel, nigga!"

"We haven't had any hoes in here, Curt," Flex said, lying through his teeth.

"Okay, so which one of you niggas wearing hot pink thongs? Let me know now so I can blow they shit back when I see 'em. That shit ain't going on around me!"

"Aight, we did have a couple bitches come through earlier, but—"

"If you lie about li'l shit, you'll lie about my money when it's short! I hate a liar with a passion and you know this! Clean up your act before you be flippin' burgers at Burger King, nigga!"

Snatching the bag from him, I left the trap and slammed the door. As I took a couple steps toward my car, T-Bone and a female I'd never seen before were walking down the street cheesing in each other's faces. Stopping in my tracks, I waited for him to get to the house. He was so engulfed in the bitch that he didn't notice me standing in the walkway.

"T-Bone, what up, fool?" I asked.

"Oh, um, 'sup, Curt? I didn't expect you to be here," he said, pushing the female behind him.

"Where you on your way to, fam?"

"I, um, was stopping over here to re-up so I could get an early start tomorrow. I sold all my shit earlier like flapjacks," T-Bone said proudly with his chest poked out like that shit meant anything to me.

"That's what's up. You taking shawty in with you?"

"Oh, nawl. I was only gon' go in, grab my pack, and be out," he said nervously, looking around at everything but me.

"I thought we were going inside. You told me this was yo' crib," the female said, snapping at him.

46

"Bitch, shut the fuck up! Ain't nobody asked you a damn thang!" T-Bone was pissed because ole girl busted his ass out, but I already knew the deal.

"Fuck all that, nigga. You real disrespectful for a muthafucka lying and shit. But check this out, you need to book a room because your days of staying here are over. The only thing that will be conducted outta there is making money. Don't let Flex set you up, because I already told him what the deal is."

"But Curt—"

"Ain't no ifs, ands, or buts about it. This ain't no muthafuckin' halfway house. You won't be bringing all yo' fuck buddies where I do business. You get paid more than enough money to take care of yourself. Have yo' shit out tonight. I'll be back."

I left his ass standing on the sidewalk as I climbed in my car. The female wasn't for his bullshit because she was walking down the street with her middle finger in the air. As I threw my whip in drive, my phone rang.

"Yeah, Ma?" I asked when I answered.

"Curtis, you still coming over today? I need you to bring me some prune juice because I haven't shitted in three days."

"Ma, I didn't need to know that! All you had to say was bring me some prune juice," I said, pulling away from the trap. "I'll be there shortly, aight?"

"Thank you, baby. That's why I love you. Hurry up, my stomach hurts," she said, hanging up.

As I drove towards my mom's crib, I thought about Shanell and the baby she was carrying. There wasn't a doubt in my mind the baby wasn't mine, but the way Shanell acted when Wes came to her apartment hadn't left my mind either. I was willing to do whatever until the baby arrived.

Messing around with Shanell wasn't hard at all. I would never end up in the predicament Wes was in because all I wanted from Shanell was pussy. His ass stayed after the fact and cuddled with her ass. Me, I busted a nut and threw a couple hundred dollars or a stack at her ass to keep her at bay.

Speaking of Wes, the two of us were very close back in the day. There were strong speculations that Shanell and I were fooling around before he got locked up. It was far from the truth. Wes going to prison was how me and Shanell became close. He had me going to their apartment to make sure she was good and drop off money.

Wes knew the type of nigga I was and he still picked me to check on his girl. True enough, I should've blocked all advances, but Shanell threw that pussy at me one too many times and I finally caught it. The pregnant kitty had a nigga and I couldn't leave it alone.

Dap brought his talking ass to the apartment one day and I was there. That's when everything went from sugar to shit, but I was still in the picture. Shanell started having me come over on select days, but I couldn't trip because I had a woman at home. I found out a few months later that Wes was out, but Shanell swore they were done.

Me and Wes never had a conversation about what happened. He just stopped fuckin' with me and we stayed out of each other's way. The day Wes and his wife showed up at Shanell's crib was the only time we were in close proximity in years. His bitch saved him from getting his shit rocked, but I had a feeling we were going to bump heads.

I stopped at the grocery store to get my mom's prune juice and I was in and out in no time. My phone chimed and I had a text from my girl, Alexis. Once I was seated comfortably, I read the message.

Alexis: Where are you?
Me: I'm heading to Ma's house. She needed some prune juice.
Alexis: I've been having a funny feeling all day. Be careful out there.

Instead of texting her back, I called and she answered right away. "Hey, baby."

"I just wanted you to hear for yourself that I'm good. Nothing's going to happen to me, baby. I love you. Stop worrying. Give Danae a kiss for me and tell her Daddy loves her."

"I love you too. Be safe and hurry home," she said, disconnecting the call.

It took ten minutes for me to pull up at my mom's crib. I sat staring at the house I grew up in and smiled. The alterations I had done to the house amazed me every time I came to visit. Plenty of money was put into the project after my mother refused to move out of the city. She refused to give up the house she said my father put his blood, sweat, and tears into.

Shaking the thoughts from my head, I grabbed the bag out of the passenger seat and got out. As I made my way up the walkway, I laughed at two little boys arguing over a foul while playing basketball. It took me back to the days of shooting hoops on that very street, but we used a garbage can instead of a hoop. When I took a step to go up the stairs, I heard a car door slam then my name was called.

"Aye yo, Curt!"

I turned my head slowly, seeing Wes and Dap walking toward me. Placing the bag on the bottom step, I watched their every move until they were a few feet away. *How the fuck did they know to come looking for me here?* I thought to myself.

"Let me holla at you, homie," Wes said roughly.

"What's there to talk about? You don't fuck with me," I smirked.

"I don't, but that's not why I'm here. Where's Shanell?" he asked, mugging me.

Laughing lowly, I shook my head at him. "Why you want to know where she at? I thought you said it was over between y'all. Don't you got a wife at the crib?"

Dap stepped forward and my hand automatically went to my waist, but I forgot my tool was in the damn car. His face hardened as he looked down to see if I was going to pull out on him. Wes reached out and grabbed Dap's left arm and from back in the day, I knew that was a sign that he was strapped. It was Wes's way of telling him to chill out.

"Where the fuck is Shanell was the question. All that other shit don't matter, nigga. This bitch is causing all kinds of problems and she needs to be stopped. Either you tell us where she is, or you gon' take this ass whoopin' for protecting the hoe. It's up to you!" Dap yelled.

"Man, fuck y'all," was all I got the chance to say before Dap launched at me, hitting me in the mouth.

I stumbled back against the banister of the porch and fell to the ground. Dap and Wes put hands and feet all over my ass and wasn't shit I could do to protect myself. Blood filled my mouth and the metallic taste of blood was on my tongue. My eye started swelling and the sound of my mother's voice is what stopped the beating they were dishing out.

"What the hell is going on out here? Get the fuck off my baby!" she hollered from the doorway, but they kept stomping me. "I'm calling the police!"

When she said "police", that's when they stopped whooping my ass. I could barely see out of my left eye as I struggled to stand up.

Wes grabbed me by the collar of my shirt with both of his hands. "Tell Shanell we are looking for her ass. If we find her and you're in the vicinity, we gon' fuck you up again," he said, pushing me back to the ground. They walked off and my mama came back out with the phone up to her ear.

"Weston, why would you to this? I know damn well this ain't about that shit that happened years ago. You're too old to be beefing over a good-for-nothing female. Curt don't even fuck with her stupid ass anymore! Stay away from my house and my son, you bastard!"

Wes got in the car without responding and they pulled away from my mama's house. Finally, being able to get to my feet, I wiped my mouth with the sleeve of my shirt and grabbed the bag off the stairs. My mother was requesting a police car and I shook my head no in her direction. Ignoring my gesture, she continued the call.

I made my way into the house and went to the bathroom after placing the bag on the kitchen table. Looking in the mirror, I saw they fucked me up, but they should've killed me. Whatever the fuck Shanell did, they took it out on my black ass, and I needed to find out what happened. After cleaning up, I stepped out of the bathroom and bumped into my mama.

"Curtis, what the hell have you done?" she asked.

"I didn't do nothing! I haven't had any contact with that nigga in years and he pops up here. This shit is bogus as hell, but I'm gon' find out what's going on. I'll call you later, Ma," I said, kissing her on the cheek.

"Please don't leave this house, Curtis. The police are on their way!" she screamed after me as I left her house.

Chapter 8
Shanell

I was sitting in my room listening to music when the sound of loud banging echoed off the walls of my apartment. I glanced at the time on my phone. It was a little after eight and nobody should've been at my door. I jumped out of the bed, marched to the front of the apartment, and looked out the peephole. On the other side, Curt was standing with a scowl on his face and blood on the front of his shirt. I unlocked the door and snatched it open.

"What the fuck did you do?" he asked, pushing past me.

"I didn't do shit! What are you talking about?" I asked after closing and locking the door. "And I thought we agreed that you would call before you showed up at my place."

Curt was pacing back and forth in front of the coffee table when his head swiveled in my direction. The side of his face as well as his left eye was swollen. There was a deep cut on his bottom lip and blood on the sleeve of his shirt. He looked like somebody stomped a mud hole in his ass and now he wanted to come let his frustrations out on me.

"What did you do to Wes?" he seethed.

"Wes did this to you?"

"Shanell, don't play with me, answer the muthafuckin' question! Why is Wes looking for you?" By this time, Curt was irate and his fists were balled tightly at his sides.

"Oh, maybe he's still mad about me hiding his daughter in a closet at the hospital. Or sending a doll to his house with a knife sticking out of the chest. Nah, he must've found out I drugged his ass the other day. I'm going to kill that bitch at the bar for running her mouth! That's the only way he could've found out about that."

Curt looked at me with a perplexed expression. "What's wrong with you, Shanell? You're letting this nigga drive you crazy because he no longer wants to deal with you. On top of that, you're fucking with his family! That's not how you handle that shit, man. You leave it alone and move the fuck around."

"Don't tell me what to do! I'm doing exactly what needs to be done. Wes is going to learn that he fucked over the wrong bitch!"

"You sound stupid as hell! Shanell, you are the reason y'all are not together."

"Me! You are the reason he doesn't love me anymore!"

Curt laughed for the first time since he came in, and I took that as him laughing at me. I instantly became furious, and the thought of eliminating his ass came to the forefront of my mind. I was not a joke. He was making a mockery of what I was going through and I didn't appreciate the shit.

"Are you laughing at me?" I asked seriously.

"Yes, I'm laughing at you, because you want to blame everyone but yourself. You are terrorizing the man's family and thought he wasn't gon' come for your head. I've never taken you as the stupid type, Shanell. The shit you doing is going to get you hurt. But I have a problem with everything you've done."

Curt yelled in my face and a speckle of spit landed on the tip of my nose. I wiped it off vigorously and stepped back.

"The nigga came for me because he don't know where the fuck *you* are! You involved me in something I have nothing to do with! I'm about to go because I'm killing that nigga soon as I find him."

The words Curt said resonated in my mind and I was piping hot on the inside. I'd be damned if I let him kill the love of my life. I didn't care what was going on between us, no one would ever hurt Weston King! Now if he said he was going to kill his bitch, I wouldn't have given two fucks. But Wes? Hell nawl!

"Where are you going?" I asked.

"I'm about to go holla at my homeboys. Wes and his brother jumped me, so I'm going to gather the troops to gun his ass up," Curt said, moving toward the door.

I had to think quickly on my feet because I couldn't let him do anything to hurt my baby daddy. "I'm going to ride with you," I said, slipping my feet in my shoes. "I need to go to the Walmart to pick up a couple things."

"Shanell, you have your own car! I don't have time to fuck around with you tonight," he said, opening the door.

"I've been sick all day and you didn't give me the chance to say all of that before you came in here with this Wes bullshit. You know what? Don't worry about it," I said, ushering him out of my apartment.

Curt wasted no time leaving and I closed the door behind him, but it was a front. When he exited the building, I grabbed a light jacket and my keys and ran out of my apartment, jumping in my car to follow him. After following him through the south side, I knew exactly where he was going. Turning down 60th, I took that street down to Damen so I could beat him to his trap.

I parked down the street and sat waiting for him to pull up. It took maybe fifteen minutes for him to pull up and it was past nine by that time. Curt got out of his car and stalked into the trap. Waiting in the car, I hit the steering wheel because I hadn't had a chance to get my knife out of the closet. Searching my armrest, I found a box cutter buried inside and smiled.

Twirling the blade around in my hand, I thought about Curt planning to kill Wes. The thought alone pissed me off and I wanted to kill his ass so bad. Curt came out of the trap with Flex in tow and I knew they were about to be on bullshit. I started my car and got ready to follow him wherever he was heading.

When he pulled out of the parking spot, I slowly followed. Curt's hands were waving in the air and he kept turning his head briefly toward Flex as he drove. We had been driving a few blocks before Curt pulled into a gas station. He got out of his car and went around to the side, where I knew a bathroom was in wait.

Curt was the type of nigga that didn't like to pull his dick out in the open to take a piss, so I knew this was going to be my one and only chance to get him alone. Pulling behind the building, I parked and got out of the car with my box cutter in hand. I pushed the button so the blade was out and locked it in place. I waited on the side of the wall, glancing around to make sure nobody was lurking.

I knew that side of the building was secluded because it was dark as fuck back there. The sound of the toilet flushing could be heard and then the water running in the sink. Getting in position, I was ready for his ass soon as the door opened. Curt stopped in his tracks when he saw me.

"What are you doing, following me?" he asked, surprised.

Without responding, I plunged the blade in his stomach and pulled it out before plunging it in and out repeatedly. Curt grabbed my jacket around the collar. I reached up and sliced his hand and he wailed out in pain, letting me go. Curt bent down and placed his hand over the gash in his stomach and I stabbed him in the side of his neck. A stream of blood flowed out like water and I jumped back. Curt fell against the building and I stabbed him in the face numerous times to make sure he was dead.

A car door slamming caused me to haul ass back to my car. Cutting through the alleyway, I blended in with traffic like it was nothing. I found a travel pack of Clorox wipes in the glove department and wiped down my hands to get rid of the blood. Curt should've kept his thoughts to himself.

I hooked my phone up to the Bluetooth and blasted Big Sean's *I Don't Fuck with You* all the way home. When I pulled up to my apartment, I scanned the block to make sure nobody was out because the last thing I needed was somebody seeing my shirt and jacket covered with Curt's blood. Racing into the building, I hurried and unlocked my door and went straight to the bathroom to shower. The moment took me back to the night I killed Greg's punk ass, but I felt different for some reason after killing Curt.

I scrubbed my body thoroughly under the hot stream of water. My skin was red as hell because it seemed as if I was trying to remove it from my body, hoping a new layer would grow. The vision of Curt's body slumping against the wall of the gas station brought tears to my eyes and I actually cried.

"Why did you plan to kill him, Curt?" I whispered lowly as the water ran down my back. "You should've just taken that ass whopping and left it alone. None of this had to happen."

I cried until my eyes were too dry to produce anymore tears. Finally turning the shower off, I grabbed a towel and stepped out of the tub. I walked down the hall to my bedroom and threw on a sweat suit and my sneakers. I went to the kitchen, took a small garbage bag from the pantry, and gathered the bloody clothes from the bathroom.

Once I tied the bag, I snatched my keys and ran back out of the house. I jumped in my car and drove to the park a couple blocks away from my house. There was a picnic area that had barbeque grills built in the ground. I seized the bag of clothes, popped the trunk, and got out to get the lighter fluid I had back there.

Running to the nearest barbeque pit, I dumped the whole bag inside and doused it with the lighter fluid. I patted my pockets and realized I didn't have a match. Heading back to my car, I searched the armrest and found a lighter and half a blunt. As I held the blunt between my lips, I lit it and pulled on it hard. I walked to one of the garbage cans in search of something to burn.

When I found a decent piece of paper, I twisted it tightly and put fire to the tip. I threw the burning paper into the pit and watched the clothes burn to a crisp and knew I had covered my tracks. Curt's murder would go unsolved because I wasn't telling a soul what I'd done. That was one secret I'd be taking to the grave.

Chapter 9
Tana

Justice and I sat and talked about everything that had transpired since she found out about Shanell. She was ready to fuck that woman up on sight, and I was waiting on her to give the signal to pounce. It didn't make sense to get hyped because nobody knew where the crazy bitch was. It was a damn shame Shanell had access to them, but she was untouchable. But patience was key because she was going to slip up.

Conya had called Justice's phone quite a few times since leaving, but Justice refused to talk to her cousin. It didn't matter how much I encouraged her to answer; she wouldn't listen. Faith had finally gone to sleep after being fussy and Justice took that opportunity to get some sleep, since she was going back to work the next day.

I was sitting downstairs waiting for Wes to come back so I could go home myself. Glancing at the clock, I saw that it was eight-thirty and I hoped he wouldn't be too much longer. When I turned on the television, there was a breaking news story on Channel Nine. The reporter was live at a gas station on 59th Street and they had the scene cordoned off with red police tape. That was a clear indication that someone had died. The reporter was talking and it made me grab the remote to turn the volume up.

"This scene is like one from a horror movie, Tad. The victim is a black male, early to mid-thirties, that has been basically mutilated behind this gas station." The reporter pointed behind her. "Police and forensic investigators are analyzing the crime scene."

At that moment, the door opened and in walked Wes and Donovan. I glanced up briefly before giving the news segment my undivided attention.

"There's a witness that was with the victim. Let's go over and see what he knows about what's going on." Shelly Martin, the reporter, walked over to a young man and pointed the mic in his face. "What happened here tonight?" she asked.

The guy's eyebrows furrowed at the reporter. "My friend just got murdered! Get the fuck outta my face! That shit is insensitive as hell, but all you're worried about is getting a story to make your pockets fatter! His mama hasn't even been notified yet. Hell, he is still lying on the side of the building with a sheet over his body and you're being nosy. Get away from me, bitch, before I reach out and touch you!"

Shelly's mouth dropped open and her eyes widened as the witness stormed away from her. "This is Shelly Martin from Channel Nine News, signing off." A commercial quickly replaced the live broadcast and I was still shocked that the reporter got checked on live TV.

"Wasn't that Lil Flex?" Donovan asked Wes.

"Yeah, but he is obviously not so little anymore. I wonder who the fuck got killed."

"Once the family is notified, they will definitely broadcast it on the news. We just have to wait and see," Dap said. "I'm about to make sure Tana gets home safely, so we're going to head out."

"Cool, brah. Thanks for being there today. All this shit is crazy as hell and I just want it to end. Have you decided on a date for your grand opening?" Wes asked.

"You don't ever have to thank me. It will get better soon. As far as the grand opening, the contractors are doing a magnificent job and they'll be finished soon. I will be more involved this week so if you need me, don't hesitate to hit me up. I'll never be too busy for any of y'all," Donovan said, making eye contact with me.

Rising to my feet, I walked to the door and slipped my feet into my shoes. I was tired as hell because I hadn't been to sleep since waking up earlier before our flight. Justice and I had to get up at six in the morning to make sure we didn't miss our flight home from Arizona. Sleepy was an understatement. I was bone tired and couldn't wait to get in bed.

Donovan had my jacket in his hands and I turned, slipping my arms into the sleeves. He automatically picked up my luggage and I smiled on the inside. Glancing at Wes, I nodded my head at him and walked in his direction.

"This ordeal has worn my friend out. Please take care of her, Wes. This is a lot for anyone to deal with. Justice is upstairs sleeping and she is adamant about going to work in the morning. Faith should be waking up in the next hour for her bottle, and she was given a bath before I put her to bed. Get some sleep and tell Justice I'll talk to her tomorrow."

Giving Wes a tight hug, I walked to the door with Donovan on my heels. As I reached for the driver's door of my car, Donovan's voice boomed through the quiet air. "Don't touched that door, Tana!" It startled me because I wasn't expecting him to do that.

"Why are you raising you voice at me, Dap? I've been opening this very door for the past two years on my own. I think I can handle it just fine."

He walked around the car and opened the door, stepping back. "As long as I'm around, you will never open another door on your own. You will learn after tonight that I don't care about your independence. I will be your man, in public and in private. Your provider, protector, and eventually your husband. Mark my words, Montana."

Donovan ushered me into the car and pulled the seatbelt over my chest. After kissing me on the cheek, he stood upright with a smirk on his face. "I'll follow you," he said, closing the door then placing my luggage in the backseat.

I watched him walk to his car before I started my engine and backed out of the driveway. It had been months since I'd had my kitty tampered with and she was drooling at the lips. Tyson had never made me feel that way from words. Donovan was a different breed and deep down, I wanted to know just how different.

As I merged on the expressway, I pushed the gas pedal and easily hit sixty miles an hour. Many thoughts entered my mind about what the future held for Justice. She had waited a long time to find love just for a bitter bitch to come along to tear it down. Justice also had come a long way to leave her past in the past, but this shit with these idiots was slowly bringing Jus "G" out of the box.

Whenever she was ready to rock, I would be there to roll. We were a force to be reckoned with when we were in street mode, but

I would trade my heels in for a pair of sneakers in a heartbeat, billy club in hand to slap a bitch without a second thought. I knew we were going to get into something, but when? That was the suspenseful part.

Turning into my complex, I parked in an empty spot not too far from the entrance. My phone rang and I fumbled inside my purse until my hand landed on it. By the time I pulled it out, I missed the call from Tyson but didn't give a fuck. The phone rang a second time as I opened the door to get out of the car and I declined that one. There was nothing me and Tyson had to discuss, so I didn't know why he was calling me anyway.

Donovan pulled his car into an empty spot three cars away and got out as I stepped out of my car. The way he strutted towards me put me in a daze. His bowed legs were so sexy to me, and my girl parts started thumping in my pants. The ringing of my phone broke me out of the spell I was in as my eyes zoomed in on the front of his pants.

Glancing down at the screen, I saw Tyson's name was displayed and I declined the call again. As I opened the back door to retrieve my luggage, I had to use my knee as leverage on the seat because it had fallen to the floor during my commute. I struggled to stand upright while yanking on the handle. My ass hit something and it caused dampness in my thong. Blood raced to my face and I was afraid to face him.

"Back up off me, Dap," I moaned over my shoulder.

"What did we discuss about that Dap shit, Tana?"

"Isn't that what you like to be called?" I asked, finally pulling the luggage out.

"Yeah, but that's not what *you* gon' call me," he said, smacking me hard on my left cheek.

"Owww!" I screamed, scratching my ass. "I don't have on any draws!"

I pushed my body into his. Dap took a few steps backwards and I slammed the door shut. He took the luggage from my hand and motioned toward the entrance to my building. All types of nasty thoughts filled my mind and I knew if I allowed him to accompany me upstairs, it would be a night to remember. I didn't want us to start off on a sexual level and have it mess up something that could possibly be great.

"Thanks for following me to make sure I got home safely. I can take it from here," I said, reaching for my luggage.

"Lead the way, Tana. I'm not trying to hear what you're talking about. I wouldn't be able to sleep if I didn't see you to your front door."

My heart pounded in my chest because it wasn't Donovan I was worried about. Truth be told, it was all me. The way I was leaking in my pants hadn't happened in a very long time. Donovan licked his lips and I almost had a major orgasm standing two feet away from him. Crossing my right leg in front of the left, I stood looking like a toddler that was fighting the urge to go to the bathroom.

"See, you gotta pee. Why are you still standing there instead of going to your apartment? Don't make me sling you over my shoulder. As a matter of fact, give me your keys."

"You can't carry me and the luggage," I laughed.

"Don't test me. Either you walk, or I'll carry you. Your choice."

The seriousness in his voice let me know he would attempt to do what he said. I chose to move and head up the walkway. My nerves were shot because one false move and I knew for a fact his dick would be down my throat. "Okay, Montana. Unlock the door and go inside. Say goodnight and let that be the end of it," I said to myself as I climbed the last step to my apartment.

Unlocking the door, I flipped the light switch and turned toward Donovan, who was standing outside the door. "Thank you. Drive safely and enjoy the rest of your night," I said, staring at the floor.

Donovan set my luggage inside the door and I still didn't look up at him. Placing his finger under my chin, Donovan lifted my head up with a grin on his face. "What are you acting all shy for, Tana?"

"I'm not. I just need to take a shower and get in bed. I have to work in the morning and you're preventing me from doing that."

"Is that so? Well, I won't hold you any longer," he said, licking his lips.

"Goodni—"

Before I could get the word out, Donovan covered my lips with his and there was no turning back. My pussy started dancing in my pants and "We fuckin' tonight" echoed in my head on repeat. My tongue pushed through his lips and he didn't resist. Wrapping his strong arms around my waist, Donovan palmed my ass and walked forward, guiding me back.

Using his foot to close the door, Donovan reached behind him to put the lock in place without breaking our kiss. I guess that was his way of saying he wasn't leaving, and I didn't have a problem with it at all. My hand automatically went to his belt buckle as he suckled on my bottom lip. My love box cried a river the minute his hand slid down the back of my pants, putting a stop to what I aimed to do. Donovan ran his hand up and down the crack of my ass and my knees grew weak.

"Aht aht. We ain't doing that, don't go weak on me now. All I was trying to do was taste those sweet lips, but you took things in another direction," he said in between pecks. "You still want to tell me goodnight?" he asked, playing in my snatch from the back.

"Unh unh," I moaned, lowering my forehead to his chest.

"Where's your bedroom?"

All I could do was point behind me. The way he was caressing my cat, I couldn't function. Using his free hand, Donovan lifted me into his arms and I automatically wrapped my legs around his waist. He turned left down the hall and I knew he was going towards the guest room, but at that point, it didn't matter. Without even looking for the light, Donovan eased me onto the bed, removing his hand from inside my pants.

He gripped my pants and pulled them over my hips slowly. I lifted my ass off the bed, moaning as the cool air of my apartment blew over my moist clit. Donovan pulled me by the legs after tossing my pants to the side and dropped to his knees. He planted soft kisses on the inside of my thighs and I pushed his head away.

"You don't have to do all of that, Donovan."

"Who you talking to?" he asked, swatting my hand away. "In a minute you gon' be begging me to suck harder."

His hands roamed over my inner thighs and I tried to scoot back on the bed. In my mind it was too soon, but my body wanted him to put a hurting on me. I was caught between giving up the goods or just telling him to wait it out. But Donovan had plans of his own, and I couldn't do shit about it.

He pulled me back to the side of the bed with my ass slightly hanging off the edge. The first touch of his tongue sent shivers down my spine. I tried to break free, but the grip Donovan had on my thighs prevented me from moving. His tongue caressed every crevice of my vagina and it felt so good. When his lips wrapped around my clit, my body elevated off the bed like Reagan from *The Exorcist*.

"Oh shit! Mmmm," I moaned.

My legs began to shake and cum shot from my body like a volcanic eruption. I tried to lower my legs, but Donovan was just beginning and he wasn't letting up. He cleaned up my pudding pop and went back in with a vengeance. My soul was being snatched right before my eyes as I gripped the back of his head while thrusting my pelvis into his face.

"Right there. Mmmm, yeah," I moaned loudly.

When he inserted his finger into my sacred hole, I almost passed out. I'd never let anyone invade my asshole and it was off limits. But for some reason, I allowed Donovan to take me to new heights. There were no limitations for me that night.

My breathing rhythm changed instantaneously and I was panting heavily. The dryness in my mouth had me nervous because it felt as if my tongue grew three times its original size. It was hard to gather moisture into my mouth, but the secretion of saliva built up after a while and I was relieved.

Donovan was eating my kitty and fingering my asshole at the same time. That action caused me to squirm around wildly. The feeling I was experiencing was one I'd never felt before. I knew my orgasm was near because my stomach clenched tightly and my clit swelled with every suck of his lips.

"Fuck! Oh my God! What are you doing to me?" I screamed, gyrating wildly.

Donovan sucked hard on my lady bud and I had no control over my body. The dam broke and I splashed my juices down his throat. It didn't seem to matter to him because he kept going. I wiggled out of his grasp. His finger slipped out of my ass and I wanted to curl up like a baby and suck my thumb.

The sound of Donovan's belt hitting the floor let me know he was far from done with me. I was ready for whatever he had to offer at that point. It was pitch black in the room so I couldn't see what he was working with down below, but I was convinced he wouldn't disappoint.

As he joined me on the bed, it dipped and my hands automatically caressed his stomach. His muscles were tight and he smelled so good. Donovan found my lips with no problem in the darkness. Our tongues danced to a rhythm that only we could hear and the aroma of my essence only heightened our desire for each other. Moaning into his mouth and enveloping my arms around his back, Donovan cupped the back of my head as he pried my legs open with his knee.

His mushroom head pushed into my tight opening and I gasped loudly. "Damn, you're tight than a muthafucka," Donovan whispered into my mouth. "It's time for me to mold your pussy to fit only me. This shit will forever be mine."

Donovan's girth stretched my walls and forced my juices to flow. Once he was fully in my tunnel, he lifted my legs in the crook of his arms and grinded slowly in and out of my love box. My juices leaked down my ass crack with every stroke he delivered and I exhaled. Donovan was touching places I didn't know existed, and the shit felt good as fuck.

The rhythm he had going had drool sliding from the side of my mouth. In two point five seconds, we went from making love to hardcore fucking. Donovan pushed my legs behind my head and those gymnastic days in college came back without a hitch. The only difference was that back then, I didn't have a big ass dick poking my uterus and knocking my large intestines out of the way.

I tried slowing him down by pushing my hand into his stomach, but that didn't work because he only slapped it down and held it over my head. My toes were touching the mattress and I was literally in a ball, and he was still fucking the shit out of me. Pulling his dick out, he stood over me and used the back of my thighs as leverage and fucked me straight with no chaser.

This position was new to me and I swear this nigga was trying to turn me into a stalker because he would never give another bitch this treatment. "Oh shit, I'm about to cum!" I yelled as I felt a huge orgasm building up.

"Let that shit go because I'm cummin' with you. This pussy good as fuck, baby," he said, hitting my hole harder with each stroke.

Donovan started going in and out quickly and I knew he was on the brink of cummin'. He started strumming my clit back and forth and I squirted all around his wood as my walls captured him in a headlock. My body started shaking and I had no control over my body.

"Aaaaaah, yeah! Oooooooooh, baby!" I screamed out as I continued to cum.

"Fuck, Tana," he moaned before snatching his dick out and groaning loudly. I felt something wet on my ass and I knew he was jerking his kids all over me as I lowered my legs. "I'm sorry about that, baby. I'm not wearing a hat and I'm not ready for kids. Come take a shower with me," he said, plopping down next to me.

***

I felt like I was walking on clouds the next morning when I left for work. It had been a minute since I'd rolled over with a man in my bed. Donovan worked my ass over something nice and a bitch was overly satisfied.

My students were at lunch so I had forty minutes of me time before they were due back to class. As I was grading the homework assignment from the day before, the intercom system buzzed in the room. Tilting my head to the side, I waited for whatever command was coming from the front office.

"Miss Taylor, there's a delivery for you," Melody the receptionist informed me.

Melody had to be mistaken. I hadn't ordered anything because I brought my lunch from home. Rising to my feet, I walked over to the intercom. Racking my brain, I couldn't figure out who the hell sent something to me. Tyson came to mind and I pushed the button to respond.

"Melody, are you sure? I didn't order anything today."

"Montana, come to the office, please," she replied.

"Okay, I'll be right there."

Retrieving my keys from my desk, I locked up the classroom and sashayed my way to the office. The heels I wore that day click-clacked on the floors with every step I took and the sound echoed throughout the hall. As I neared the office, Mr. Davidson was exiting the men's bathroom. A smile spread across his face when he laid eyes on me.

"Good afternoon, Miss Taylor."

"Good afternoon," I said without pausing.

"Damn, Montana. When are you going to give me a chance? I've been chasing you for years," he said, following me down the hall. "What will it take for you to go out with me?"

I turned to face him because he was really getting on my nerves. He wasn't taking anything I'd said in the past seriously. Before I could respond, a voice bellowed out behind me.

"If you cut your arm off, sacrifice your first born, or offered her a million dollars, you still wouldn't stand a chance, homie. Montana has all the man she needs right here. Don't you got a room full of kids that came to school to learn? They can't achieve that if you're out hear hounding my woman."

My heart was beating as if I had run three miles around the track behind the school. I slowly pivoted my feet around. The murderous glare Donovan had trained on Mr. Davidson had me nervous. Not knowing what his next move would be, I walked up to him and stood on my toes, planting a passionate kiss on lips. Donovan wrapped his arms around my waist, deepening the kiss.

Breaking the kiss, Donovan looked into my eyes and smiled, but it didn't last long when his eyes shifted behind me. "You still standing there? Take yo' ass on, Patna. This is all me," he chuckled.

"You got it," Mr. Davidson said. I few seconds later, the sound of his footsteps could be heard walking away. I glanced up at Donovan and he was still staring down the hall.

"What are you doing here?" I asked, bringing his attention back to me.

"I was on my way to Customs by Dap II and figured I'd come see the woman that rocked my world last night," he smirked.

"Awww, that was sweet of you."

Donovan grabbed my hand and led me to the office. He allowed me to enter first and my mouth dropped open. There were two dozen roses, a bottle of white grape apple cider, and a small box on the counter. Tilting my head back, my eyes met his and he encircled his arms around my waist and kissed my forehead.

"Thank you so much!" I smiled. Stepping closer to the counter, I sniffed the flowers and picked up the bottle of cider. "Why did you buy me an adult juice bottle?"

"Tana, I couldn't bring anything that contained alcohol into your work place. Don't worry, I'll have the good stuff with me when I come see you tonight. If that's alright with you."

Standing with my finger pressed against my cheek like I was thinking about what he said, I smiled. "That sounds good. We can sip a little something while you help me grade the papers I'll be bringing home with me."

"You got me fucked up, Tana. You the teacher, baby. But you know what? I'll make an exception for you," he said, reaching around me for the box that I didn't touch purposely. "I got this for you. I hope you like it."

Slowly easing the wrapping off, my hands shook and the box fell to the floor. I didn't know why I was nervous, but I felt like a teenager on her first date. Donovan bent down and picked it up and handed it back to me.

"Now open the box, Tana. There's more to come. You just have to allow me to spoil you."

"You don't have to buy me things, Donovan. I can do that on my own," I said, tearing the rest of the paper off.

Inside was a black box with the Customs by Dap logo on the top of the lid. I lifted it and the most beautiful charm shined in my eyes. Donovan took the box from me and took the item out. When he raised the platinum chain up for me to see, the charm was glistening with diamonds and I loved it. I had never seen anything like it before. It read "Queen of Customs" with a crown sitting on the Q. I was curious as to why he would get the charm for me.

When I looked up, Donovan had pulled his chain from his shirt and he had the same one, but his said, King of Customs. Once I saw that, I knew exactly what he was trying to say, but how? We had only known each other a short time. Yes, we had sex, but that didn't amount to us being together.

The shit Tyson put me through made it hard for me to even think about jumping into another relationship. Donovan was a great guy and the chemistry was definitely there between us, but I wanted us to get to know one another in every way possible before we jumped into anything. It was too soon for gifts of that magnitude.

"It's beautiful," I said, eyeing the chain he still held in his hand. "But I can't accept that, Donovan."

"You can and you will. We don't have to put any titles on anything. I already know what I want and I'm a spoiled nigga so that should tell you that I get what I want, eventually. There's nothing to worry about. I won't stalk you like your schoolboy crush back there," he said, turning me around before draping the chain around my neck.

The charm fell between my breasts and I instantly looked down at it. The sound of children chattering made me remember I was at work. My assistant was passing the office door when she doubled back and peeked inside.

"Oooweee, Boss Lady. He is fine," she said, sticking her tongue out at me.

I laughed, shaking my head. "Take them to the room. Here's the key. Start them on Chapter 8 in the math book and I'll be there shortly."

She walked over, giving Donovan a once over and whispered, "I hope you're better than that other fool."

"Yeah, he fucked up, shawty. Ain't no coming back," Donovan said, planting a kiss on my lips. The ohhs and ahhs from the kids had me blushing. "Let me get out of here. I'll see you later to help with grading those papers."

He kissed me once more and headed for the exit. My eyes were glued on the door long after he left and I was in a daze. Melody cleared her voice, bringing me back to reality.

"I think he's a good one. Give him a chance, Montana, just take it slow."

"Thank you. I have a lot to think about for sure," I said, gathering my gifts off the counter.

"Your boo ain't gon' like that shit one bit," She laughed.

"Girl, he already had to pick his face off the floor before I made it to the office. That's a story for another day though. I have to get back to my kids." I giggled.

"Oh lawd, Tana. That fine ass man hurt his feelings. No more lunch for you."

"Girl, shut up," I said, walking out the office.

The day went by quickly after Donovan's visit and the clock struck three before I realized it. "Okay, class. Make sure you have your math and history books in your bookbags because I don't want to hear any excuses about anyone not having their homework tomorrow. The extra credit assignment is pages sixty-six through seventy-seven in your math textbooks. It's an easy task to raise your grade. Enjoy the rest of your day."

When the last child exited my room, my assistant lingered around a bit longer than usual, but I had no plans of talking to her about my personal life. She must've caught on, because she said goodbye and left a few minutes later.

I was rushing to get out of the building because I didn't want to run into Mr. Davidson. Nearing the exit, I saw him in the office and made a dash out the door as fast as my heels would go.

As I hit the key fob to unlock the door to my car, my phone rang loudly. My hands were too full to even attempt to answer it. After placing the flowers on the backseat and the apple cider and my briefcase on the floor, I closed the door, climbing into the driver seat. I put my purse on the passenger seat and dug around for my phone. As soon as I unlocked the screen, it began to ring again. Tyson's name was on display and I sighed long and hard before answering.

"Hello," I said, turning the key in the ignition.

"I know your ass saw me calling you last night, Tana!"

I took the phone away from my ear and looked at it to make sure it was Tyson on the other end. Pushing the button to connect the call to the Bluetooth, I put the phone in the cup holder.

"Do you hear me talking to you?"

"First of all, who the fuck you think you're talking to, Tyson?" I asked, backing out of the parking space.

"I'm talking to you! Why didn't you answer the phone when I called you last night? What were you doing that was more important?"

I chuckled because his ass sounded like a fuckin' clown. "I didn't answer because obviously you weren't who I wanted to talk to last night. I'm not obligated to answer when you call my phone, Tyson. We are no more. When are you going to realize when you told me we were done, that's all that needed to be said?"

"What if I told you I didn't want that anymore?"

"Then you will be saying that shit for the hell of it, because it will never happen. I don't go backwards. There are no second chances when it comes to a fuck nigga trying to play with my heart. Go play with Rachel. She may want to play this stupid ass game you niggas invented. The shit won't work on me."

The line was quiet for a long while and I thought Tyson had hung up. I didn't bother to check and make sure. Instead, I continued to drive through the heavy afternoon traffic. My mind went back to the night before and the lovemaking session Donovan and I had. I was smiling from ear to ear until Tyson's voice filled my car.

"Tana—"

"Fuck, I thought you hung up!" I yelled.

"You act like I'm getting on your fuckin' nerves or something. I'm only trying to let you know I miss you. We have too much history to just call it quits, Tana. I want to make it up to you, baby, because you deserve the best and I'm willing to do whatever it takes."

Listening to his ass get his baby, baby Keith Sweat on, I laughed hard as hell in my head, but when I opened my mouth, it was a different tune that came out.

"You *are* getting on my fuckin' nerves! You are like a gnat that won't go the fuck away, Tyson. The only reason you want me back is because the bitch you left me for allowed her family to make decisions for her. I knew what I wanted when I was with you. It was *you* that thought there was something better out there for your ass. Like the saying goes, the grass wasn't greener on the other side, huh?"

A car swerved in front of me and I pressed hard on the horn. "Stupid muthafucka, stay yo' ass over there and learn how to drive, hoe!" I screamed as I tried to see the person in the car. The hoe knew she was wrong and refused to look at me.

"Are you alright, Tana?" Tyson asked.

"Why are you still on my phone, Tyson? I'm going to say this for the last time, we are done! We will never be together again, so there's no sense in you continuing to try. I loved you at one point, but you showed me I deserve better. I'm ready to let my hair blow in the wind while I mingle, because a bitch is single. Bye, Tyson."

I hung up on his ass and told Siri to play Jill Scott. I sang *Golden* all the way home because I was about to be living my life like it was golden from that point on.

Chapter 10
Justice

Life in the King household was getting a lot better. Things had been rough in the beginning, but it was mellowing out. Wes had been giving me space because of all the drama with Shanell. When he came home the night of the baby shower, he told me what happened and I couldn't believe the depth Shanell went through to get at him. It had been quiet for the past week and in the back of my mind, I knew there was something brewing in the background.

I missed my baby the first couple of days, but it had gotten a lot easier being away from her. Beverly was always ready when I dropped Faith off in the morning. She would be waiting in the window as soon as I pulled up into the driveway then come outside to stand on the porch as I got the baby out of the car. Beverly was a trip because she wouldn't even allow me to kiss my own damn baby before she was shooing me away from her house.

It felt good to be back at work. The day I returned I was tired as hell because the night before was a pretty restless one for me. I was lost as hell because I'd been off work for a couple months, but I got back in the groove within an hour or two of being on the clock. My ass had a baby and that shit didn't affect the scholar I was born to be. The manager I worked hard to be was back.

The day was dragging and I had just finished counting sixty-nine thousand, five hundred and forty-five dollars by hand. I didn't want to see another fuckin' bill in my life. As I walked from the back vault, Valerie, one of my best tellers, met me in the middle of the lobby.

"Justice, girl, it's boring in here today," she said, looking around the bank.

"What do you want, Val?" I chuckled. The way Valerie was set up, she was easing in slowly because she had a story to tell. There wasn't enough time in the day for her to take her time, so I had to rush her along.

"Justice, when you left yesterday, there was a crazy ass bitch that came up in here asking about you."

At that point, she had my undivided attention because I wanted to know who the fuck she was talking about. My eyes furrowed and my head slightly jerked back.

"Don't look at me like that. Let me tell you what happened."

"Well talk, Valerie," I said irritably.

When she opened her mouth to say something, the door to the entrance opened and my cousin Conya walked in. I hadn't talked to her since she left my house the night of my baby shower. Conya looked around the lobby until she spotted me, then walked slowly toward me. Hopefully, for her sake, she wasn't coming to my job on bullshit because I didn't have a problem fucking her up.

"Hold that thought, Valerie. Is that the person that came in looking for me?" I asked.

"No, that's not the woman. Do you know her?"

"Yeah, that's my cousin. I'm about to talk to her in my office. If you need anything, go to Matt."

Conya finally made it across the lobby. My cousin was beautiful, but for some reason, she didn't think so. I guess because she was what most consider a big girl, she had low self-esteem. Everybody tried to let her know that her size didn't matter, but she never wanted to hear the shit. The pantsuit she had on looked good on her.

"Hey, Justice," she said, standing in front of me.

"What's up, cousin? I'm surprised to see you on this side of town. What brings you by?"

"I wanted to apologize for what I said to you. I was wrong," she said sincerely.

"Follow me. This is a conversation that needs to be discussed in private. I don't need anyone in my business."

I led the way to my office, and Conya followed behind me. As I rounded the corner, Matt was coming out of his office. He nodded in my direction and kept going down the hall. When we got to my office, I stepped to the side, allowing Conya to enter first. Motioning for her to have a seat, I sat in the chair behind my desk, wasting no time getting back to the subject at hand.

"Yes, you were wrong. There's a time and place for one to speak on their opinion, Conya. You could've called me and said all the bullshit that came out of your mouth. To me, it seemed like you were trying to embarrass me. That was the reason I clapped back the way I did."

Conya's head lowered and she started shifting in her seat.

"Bringing up shit from my past was a hoe move. I was young as hell and didn't know how that love shit worked. Yeah, I got played, but the shit going on in my life now is different from the puppy love back then. You went hard as if you had something to prove."

"It's not that at all, Justice," Conya said, raising her head up. "When we were younger, every boy flocked to you. It was like I was overlooked because your beauty didn't give room for anybody to notice me."

"Let me stop you right there. I've always told you to lift your head and own yo' shit, Conya. I had no control over a nigga not approaching you. None of that had anything to do with me. You were hating on me so hard yo' tongue got thicker than a muthafucka every time you talked about me."

There was no way I was about to let her use me as a scapegoat for her own insecurities. If I didn't want her around me, I wouldn't have invited her anywhere I would be. Conya needed to hear what I was saying and leave it alone so we could move on with our lives. Tears escaped her eyes, but she didn't utter a vowel.

"I never disliked you. Hell, we're family, and you know how I feel about blood. For you to say I needed you when I got my heart broken was a shot, but you can have that. Next time, mention how I was always there for you when a bitch and her friends were always whoopin' that ass. Even though you had done some fucked up shit, I still stood by your side. I never tried to front about what I'd done for you and I won't start now."

Conya sniffed as she wiped her face, but I had no sympathy for her. All I could do was grab a couple tissues and hand them to her so she could catch the snot before it touched her lip. She gladly took them from my hand and cleaned her face.

"I'm sorry if I hurt you, Justice. I want to be able to watch my little cousin grow up and have a relationship with you in the process," Conya said in between sniffles.

"You don't have to be sorry, but I want you to be mindful of what you say. I've given you many chances when we were kids. That shit isn't going to fly in this day and age. I'm here to let you know, I will beat the fuck out of you if you ever come at me like that again. I will forget we are related. You of all people know how I am when a muthafucka tries to wrong me."

Getting up from my seat, rubbing the creases out of my skirt, I walked to the door and held it open. That was an indication to her that the conversation was over. I didn't want to hear shit else about it because I let it go just that fast. "I have work to do, but we can go out for drinks soon if you want."

"I understand, and I should've called before I came, but this has been on my mind since it happened. Justice, I know you, and it takes a long time for you to forgive somebody. Hopefully you will forgive me wholeheartedly," Conya said, standing to her feet.

"Girl, shut your ass up. I said I accept your apology. Don't piss me off and get your ass whooped in here. Come on so I can get back to the business that pays me."

As I walked out of my office, Valerie was hurrying down the hall fast. My first thought was she had to use the bathroom badly, but when she stopped in front of me, I knew it was something else. She looked up at me then at Conya without saying anything.

"Valerie, what's wrong with you?"

"Remember when I was telling you a woman came in looking for you?"

"Yes."

"Well, she's here. Matt is talking to her and she's making a huge scene in the lobby. She said something about you stealing her man and you better come out and face her like a woman."

I let her words marinate and Shanell came to mind instantly. Heading back to my office, I sat behind my desk as Valerie and

Conya appeared in the doorway. I kicked off my heels, reached under my desk and grabbed my Nikes. Once I had the shoes on my feet, I put my hair in a ponytail and made my way to the lobby.

"Justice, please don't allow this woman to jeopardize your job," Valerie said, speed walking to stay beside me.

"If this is who I think it is, you have no clue what she's put me and my family through. Fuck this job!" Rounding the corner, I could hear Shanell before setting my eyes on her. Matt and the security guard were trying to get her out of the door, but she spotted me and broke away from them.

"Just the bitch I was looking for," Shanell said, running up on me. "I knew if I kept coming here, you would stop hiding and show your face."

She swung and connected with my jaw. That was my go ahead to mop her ass across the floor of that bank. I didn't even flinch when she hit me and before I knew it, we were knocking shit over because I was trying to tear her head off her body. The way we were fighting in the middle of the lobby, one would've thought they were watching a heavyweight boxing match.

I hadn't fought a bitch that could hang with me blow for blow since I was young, but I wasn't trying to back down from the challenge she brought upon me. Matt and Charles tried to separate us, but I had that bitch's hair clasped in my hand, serving her ass knuckle sandwiches. The uppercuts I delivered to her mouth caused her to leak blood all over the floor. Charles snatched Shanell by her waist and I heard her hair rip from her scalp.

"Arrgh, you bitch!" she screamed, trying to free herself from Charles's grasp. "You will never live happily ever after with him, bitch! I will make your life a living hell long as I live."

"I'm glad you feel that way, because every time you run up on me, I'm going to have an ass whooping prepared for that ass. Choose your muthafuckin' battles, bitch. I'll be ready for your ass the next time too."

Charles was holding on to her tightly when the doors to the bank swung open. Two uniformed cops walked in with their hands on their guns. One walked over to Shanell and handcuffed her immediately. The other officer came toward me and Matt stopped him in his tracks.

"Justice wasn't the aggressor. She only defended herself," he said, talking to the officer. "She was here doing her job when that woman came in screaming and hollering. I don't know what the problem is, but something is very wrong with her."

The officer turned his attention to me, "Ma'am, what happened?" he asked.

"Bitch, I got something for you," Shanell laughed, showing her bloodstained teeth. "I'm going to kill your ass next time."

"I'm not worried about your bum ass! You're just mad because the nigga you took for granted don't want yo' ass—"

"Don't say anything to her! Grady, take her to the car," the officer yelled.

Officer Grady led Shanell out of the building and everyone went back to what they were doing. Matt stayed by my side and Conya appeared on the other side.

"Who is that woman and what is all of this about?"

"Can we go into my office and talk about this? It's kind of personal and don't want any more of my business on display," I said seriously.

"Sure, lead the way," the officer said.

As I led the way to my office, I thought about how much I despised the police and didn't trust them at all. The last thing I wanted to do was talk to them about Shanell, but I knew there was no way around it. I wished they were never called, but somebody in the building must've gotten scared when Shanell threw the first punch. Once again, I sat in the chair behind my desk and waited for Matt and the officer to take a seat.

Conya tried to enter and was stopped at the door. "We don't need you here, ma'am," the officer said. "You can leave now."

"That's my cousin in there," Conya proclaimed.

"I understand, but I want to talk to her to get some insight as to what's going on."

Conya being there was unnecessary and I didn't really want her to get in a catfight with the police. Standing from my seat, I went to the door and spoke over the officer's shoulder. "Conya, I'll call you later. Let me handle this situation with the police."

She stood there for a minute before nodding and walking off. I went back to the desk and sat down as the officer closed the door. Matt sat quietly, waiting for the officer to start his questioning as I was. The officer took a seat and sighed loudly.

"Okay, let's start from the top. I'm Officer Johnson. Tell me what's going on."

"Well, the woman that you arrested is, Shanell Jones. She used to be in a relationship with my now-husband, Weston King, and she isn't too happy about it. Shanell has been giving us hell the last couple months and I'm so over it," I explained reluctantly.

"What exactly has she done, Mrs. King?"

"I want you to know up front my husband played a part in how Shanell is acting. She trashed the apartment that he paid the bills on when he told her she had to move out. That was minor compared to what she has done afterwards. She came to the hospital and hid my newborn daughter in a closet!"

Thinking about how I could've lost Faith had me emotional and tears clouded my vision. Snatching a tissue from the box on my desk, I dabbed the corners of my eyes before continuing. I gathered myself and I took a deep breath.

"When the police came to my room to take a statement, they said there wasn't enough proof that Shanell was involved, even though she sent a message to my husband stating she did."

Officer Johnson was jotting in a notebook as I spoke and when he finished, he glanced up at me. "Did your husband give the message and number to the officers?"

"We gave them the number but unfortunately, Shanell used a burner phone and the number was disconnected, so there was no way to say it was actually her. There were other things that occurred as well. She sent a doll to my home and it looked just like my daughter. The creepy thing about it was the fact that she had embedded a knife in the chest of the doll, along with a note stating she could've killed my child."

The tears fell onto my hand and I wiped them off my face quickly. Anger was building up and I wanted to fuck her up again because I felt the fight wasn't enough. Murder was on my mind and I wanted to carry the task out.

"Did you report that to the police?" Officer Johnson asked, taking notes.

"Actually, we didn't, because I feel the police isn't doing anything about the situation. Shanell has been able to contact us and invade our personal space, but we don't know where the hell she is. To me, the police isn't taking any of the things she has put us through serious enough."

"To be honest with you, Mrs. King, the lack of evidence plays a major role in the way we do our job. We have her for assault here today and she threatened you in front of an officer."

"But what about her vandalizing my husband's car and drugging him so she could have sex with him?" I said, getting that little bit of information out.

"Were the police called for those incidents?"

"Wes has a police report about the vandalism and the police have a copy of the surveillance video too. As far as her drugging him, he found out it was her when he went back to the bar where it took place. Shanell was identified as the person that 'helped' him get home," I said, bending my index and middle fingers on both hands.

Officer Johnson wrote in his notebook and closed it when he was finished. "Mrs. King, you aren't being arrested because there were witnesses that Miss Jones attacked you. I want you to stay clear of her. She will be in lockup for the remainder of the day, but if we have nothing to hold her on, she will be out again."

I was upset that he was telling me to stay away from Shanell even though I'd already told him that Wes and I don't have access to the bitch. On top of that, the bitch could be out of jail in less than twenty-four hours and that didn't sit well with me. She was danger-ous, and that wasn't what I was worried about because I knew how to defend myself against anything.

"You do not have to constantly tell me to stay away from her. If you were listening to anything I've said, you would already know, she is bringing bullshit our way. I'm all for staying away from her, but she has to stay the fuck away from me. I can't make any prom-ises about what will happen if she comes after me or my family again."

"I understand what you're saying, Mrs. King," Officer Johnson said, rising to his feet. "This incident will be on file and I'll keep in touch. If I have any further questions, I'll contact you. Until then, don't hesitate to call me if anything else comes to mind."

Officer Johnson placed a card on my desk and I gave him one of my business cards in return. He left out of my office and it was just Matt and myself in the room. A part of me was embarrassed because it was very unprofessional for me to act the way I did at work, but I didn't have a choice in the matter. I knew I was going to get reprimanded for my actions, but I didn't care.

"Justice, I know what happened wasn't your fault," Matt said, clearing his throat. "I don't want to fire you for this, but I will have to give you a few days of suspension. The incident was unavoidable, but I don't want others to think it's okay to carry on the same way. You are a manager and you are in a position where you are looked up to. I'm not upset at you, so don't think that's the case at all."

I sat listening to what he was saying and I understood his point. Maybe being home a little longer wasn't a bad idea, and I was really looking forward to being with Faith during the day. I wanted all of this shit to stop so I could live life with my family.

"Is it possible for me to use the rest of my maternity days?" I asked.

"I'm not supposed to do something like that, but I'm not going to put anything in the system. This has to stay between the two of us because we can both lose our jobs over this shit. You can have the three weeks that you didn't take. If you need anything, don't hesitate to call me. I'm here for you, Justice."

Matt stood and reached across the desk and squeezed my hand. "Protect your home, Justice. From what I heard, that broad is crazy as hell. Watch yourself, because she's going to try you again. To be honest, I thought you were a good girl," he laughed. "You beat her ass!"

"Never judge a book by its cover, Matt. There's a lot you don't about me," I smirked.

"I see that shit now. Go home and enjoy your vacation. Don't get in any trouble, okay?"

"Tell trouble don't come my way and I'll be alright."

Matt shook his head as he turned to leave.

"Thanks for having my back, Boss. I really appreciate it," I called out behind him.

He waved without turning around and left. I gathered my belongings and left my office, wondering what I would do for the next three weeks since I couldn't come back to work. I was grateful to still have a job after the bullshit Shanell's bitch ass pulled.

Chapter 11
Shanell

"Why the fuck y'all locking me up? You see what she did to my face?"

I was mad because these stupid-ass pigs cuffed my ass fast as hell. I put my foot in my mouth by saying I was going to kill that hoe Justice next time I saw her. And I meant that shit too.

"You're going to jail for assault for sure and trespassing if the bank press charges on you, ma'am. Don't say another word until we get to the station," Officer Johnson said as he pulled into traffic.

I was trying to wiggle my way out of the cuffs, but they had them muthafuckas on too damn tight. After a while I just sat back and enjoyed the ride because they didn't have shit to hold me on and I'd be out in the morning. The first time I went to the bank, Justice wasn't there, but I knew she couldn't hide for too long. My plan was to keep showing up until I caught her ass and the day finally presented itself.

What I wasn't prepared for was the fact her hands felt like lethal weapons. When I hit her, it didn't seem to faze her one bit. But when she hit my ass, I could've sworn I saw Tweety bird flying in front of my eyes. It felt like I got knocked upside the head by a fuckin' man. There was no way I was going to stop swinging because had I done that, the paramedics would've been carrying me out on a stretcher.

The squad car pulled into the parking lot of the police station and I waited patiently for them to open the door. The officer got out of the driver's side and Officer Grady followed, coming to the back door. I was roughly pulled out, and that shit didn't sit well with me.

"You don't have to rough handle me! It's bad enough these damn cuffs are cutting into my wrists," I yelled angrily, planting my feet on the ground.

"Lower your tone, because you are the reason you're here. Getting mad at me won't help your situation. What did you think, you were going to get the royal treatment? If so, you thought wrong. Now walk!"

I was damn near dragged into the building and placed in an empty room and cuffed to a chair. Officer Grady left and I was alone, wondering why I wasn't put in lockup. My hand started going numb from the pressure on my wrist and it only pissed me off even more.

Wes was at fault for all of this shit. If he hadn't led me on, none of us would be going through any of this. But since he wanted to play with fire, his ass was going to burn. I had something for his ass, and he was going to wish he hadn't played with my mutha-fuckin' emotions when I was finished with him.

The door opened after what felt like forever and Officer Grady and his partner walked in and closed the door. The darker officer slapped a folder on the table and stared at me as if it was going to scare me. I didn't know what was in the folder, but I was ready.

"Shanell Jones, I'm Officer Johnson. I have a couple things I would like to discuss with you."

Rolling my eyes, I shifted to the side and propped my elbow on the arm of the chair. Clearing his throat, Officer Johnson folded his hands in front of him. "Why were you at the bank today, Miss Jones?"

"Why do you go to the bank, *Officer Johnson*?" I chuckled.

"I'm not in the mood for your bullshit, Miss Jones. Why were you at the bank?"

Putting on my serious face, but still laughing on the inside, I leaned forward. "I went there to confront the bitch that stole my man from under my ass," I said, sitting back in the chair.

"Miss Jones, why do you think that was a good idea?" Officer Johnson asked.

"I wanted to know why she felt the need to go after my man! Fuck you mean! Wes belonged to me! So, I needed to see her to beat her ass!"

"Well, Miss King told us a few different stories about how you have been disrupting her and Mr. King's lives. I would like to hear your side of the story now. First, have you been harassing the Kings?" he asked.

"Nope," was the only response I gave.

"Did you send a doll to the King's house?"

"I don't even know where he lives, let alone send something to their house. Where did you get that from?"

"So, you're trying to tell me you have no idea where they live? If you start lying, you will make this harder for yourself, Miss Jones," Officer Johnson said sternly.

"Okay, I know where they live, but I never sent anything to their house! What I won't do is keep repeating myself. I didn't do that shit."

"What about hiding their daughter at the hospital?"

"Fuck Justice! The bitch is trying to get me locked up on some shit she made up and you're believing every word she said. I'm here to tell you none of that shit is true. If I wanted to do anything to anybody, I could. But I don't see y'all saying anything about her fuckin' my face up."

Both of the officers looked at me with blank stares. If I wasn't confined to the chair, I would've attacked them muthafuckas. Officer Johnson opened the folder in front of him and shifted through the papers. When he found what he was looking for, he pushed the paper towards me.

"Weren't you institutionalized when you were a teenager, Miss Jones?"

Reading over the document, my eyes bulged because I never thought my past would come back to haunt me. My hand started shaking uncontrollably so I sat on it so the pigs wouldn't notice how nervous I was. When I read the description of how Greg was found, my body instantly calmed and I had to suppress the giggle that tickled my throat.

"Do you want to take us back to the day in question, Shanell?"

Moving my eyes from the paper over to Officer Grady, the saliva in my mouth built up fast but I swallowed it. In order to get out of there, I knew I couldn't act on impulse. Gritting my teeth together, I growled lowly because they were trying to interrogate me on something that happened so many years before and I wasn't with that shit.

"No, I don't want to talk about any of that. Are we here to talk about what happened today, or are y'all gon' try to incriminate me on some shit I already served time for?" I barked.

"All we're trying to do is figure out what your mindset was back then. There's no need for you to get upset," Officer Johnson replied.

"I'm quite sure you read the bullshit in the report. The story my mother came up with was a lie because she wasn't even home when the shit happened. Greg's nasty dick ass raped me and he was the fuckin' victim because I protected myself by slitting his fuckin' throat! Get the fuck outta my face!" I said, rising to my feet bringing the chair along with me.

"Miss Jones, sit down!" Officer Johnson yelled, jumping up. "We need to hear your side of the story. That's all."

Sitting back down, the cuff banged against my wrist, but the pain didn't affect me. The scowl didn't leave my face, and it felt like my shit was smothered in concrete. That's how hard I was eyeing them muthafuckas.

"I already pleaded my case when I was sixteen years old! I'm not reliving that shit because that was when my life changed. I lost my mama and was left to fend for myself because she decided to believe the man she was fuckin' would ever touch her own daughter! I'm not going through that shit again. You can lock me up now because it's obvious that y'all don't have shit on me other than assault." I giggled, trying too hard not to lash out. "Y'all fishing now, but take me to a cage so I can go to sleep and be outta this bitch tomorrow." I laughed and sat back. I would've crossed my arms, but I couldn't due to the fact of being restrained to the chair.

"Take her to one of the cells, Grady. She's not going to say anything else."

Officer Johnson was pissed, but I didn't give a fuck. He didn't have shit on me and I'd be out of that bitch sooner than later.

After cuffing both of my hands behind my back, Officer Grady led me through the station and put me in a cell by myself before he

uncuffed me. He stood watching as I sat on the bench, getting com-
fortable. I didn't pay his ass no attention, but my mind was going
thirty miles an hour thinking about what I was going to do when I
was released. Justice thought she got the best of me, but I was about
to make many people cry at once.

Chapter 12
Wes

I got off work early and couldn't wait to pick my baby up from my mama's. Justice was going to be surprised because I had plans to cook dinner, run her a hot bath, and give her a full body massage before I blessed her with this pipe. It had been a minute since we'd had any type of body to body contact and I was ready to caress my wife's body sensually.

As I neared my parents' block, my phone rang. Glancing down at the screen, Justice's picture was on display and it caused me to smile. Without hesitation, I pushed the button to connect the call.

"Hey, baby," I said as I maneuvered down the street.

"You driving?"

"Yeah, I got off early. I'm on my way to get Faith from Mom. I want to pamper you tonight, baby, you deserve it."

"That sounds so nice, but I'm already at your parents' house and you need to get here quickly."

"Justice, I'm right down the street, is everything alright?" I asked, pressing down on the gas pedal. "Are you sick or something? Because you're off work mighty early."

"There's a couple detectives here saying they got a tip that you killed Curt." Her voice shook and she sounded like she was on the verge of crying.

"Whoever gave them a tip lying! I haven't killed no damn body! I'll be pulling into the driveway in a minute," I said, disconnecting the phone.

My heart was racing because I hadn't seen or heard from Curt since me and Dap beat his ass. We didn't inflict enough damage to kill that nigga, I know for a fact. But hearing Justice say the police were at my parents' crib on a bogus-ass tip had me paranoid as hell. As I signaled to make a left turn, I called Dap.

"Where you at, bro?" he said lowly when he answered.

"I'm pulling up to Pops' house. How fast can you get there?"

"You late. I'm already here. I'll see you when you get here," he said, hanging up.

I parked on the street and got out. My feet felt like dead weight, but I shook that shit off because I hadn't done anything. There was no reason for me to kill Curt, especially not over some pussy, Shanell's pussy at that. Reaching the top of the stairs, I motioned to ring the bell and the door opened. My father stood with a worried expression on his face.

"What the fuck have you done?" he whispered.

"Nothing—"

"Weston King?" a tall black man said, walking over to where me and my father stood.

"Yes?" I replied, entering my parent's home. "What's this all about?" I asked, making eye contact with Justice as she sat feeding Faith on the couch.

"I'm Detective Roman and this is my partner Detective Barnett. We need to ask you a few questions about your altercation with Curtis Miles."

"There's nothing to say. I whooped his ass and that's all there is to it," I said, taking a seat in my father's recliner.

"Unfortunately, that's not all there is to it, Mr. King. We have witnesses that you and your brother assaulted Mr. Miles in front of his mother's house February 16th at approximately 7:30 p.m."

"I just told you I beat that nigga's ass. The timeframe fits. You and your witness would be accurate about what happened. His mother called the law as we were leaving. Tell me something I don't know. I'm not denying the fact that I put hands on him. We fought, he fell, and we left. Simple as that," I said truthfully.

"It's ironic for you to admit getting into an altercation with Mr. Miles and he turns up dead a little over an hour later. He was gutted like a fish behind a gas station on 59th Street with his face still battered from your assault," Detective Barnett's voice boomed through the room, startling Faith.

"Baby, take Faith into the other room, please," I said, staring the detective down. Once Justice left the room, I went in on his ass. "Just because I beat Curt's ass automatically makes me a murderer? Bullshit! The only thing I'm guilty of his putting my hands on him.

As far as killing somebody, one thing I can tell you is I would never use a sharp object to get the job done."

"Where were you at approximately 8:30 p.m., Mr. King?" Detective Roman asked.

"I was at home watching the live news report on the murder at the very gas station you mentioned," I said, pausing briefly. "As a matter of fact, when I was watching the segment, I recognized a dude that used to run the streets with us back in the day giving the news reporter hell. To be honest, I didn't know who was killed because a name hadn't been released. This is the first I've heard about it being Curt."

Dap stepped forward with his arms folded over his chest. Both of the detectives turned, glancing in his direction. Licking his lips, Dap put his arms down and rubbed his hands together.

"Check this out. There is no denying we got into it with Curt, but neither me nor my brother had anything to do with his murder. I'm quite sure there is surveillance at the gas station that you can look at. We were nowhere near the vicinity. I have proof that I was in the suburbs after eight o'clock because I stopped at the gas station to fill up and grab a bottled water."

Dap pulled his phone out of his pocket and tapped a couple times on the screen. After pulling up whatever he was looking for, he handed his phone to the detective. As Detective Roman studied the information Dap provided, we all waited for him to respond.

"What is this?" he asked.

"This is proof me and brother was not in the city at the time of this crime. We were at the gas station on 167th and Pulaski. I stopped to fill up my tank and bought a bottled water." Dap repeated the statement again to make sure the detectives registered what he said.

"The cameras at the location were not working, so we have nothing to obtain from the gas station. You two are the prime suspects in this investigation until we can prove otherwise."

Dap ignored what he said and pointed at the phone. "This is a receipt from the Shell gas station. Both me and Wes went inside so if you go there, I guarantee their cameras work. I refuse to go down for some shit we had nothing to do with. Investigate at all costs, because y'all barking up the wrong tree."

Detective Ramon gave Dap back his phone and looked back and forth between the two of us, "Don't leave town. We may have more questions for you or simply to place you under arrest." He smirked as he headed for the door. "Y'all have a nice day now."

Once they were gone, my mama jumped on our asses like white on rice. "What the fuck did y'all do! Got the police in my mutha-fuckin' house and shit talking about murder! Y'all know damn well I smoke weed, and for them to show up out of the blue had my ass scared to death."

"Weed is legal here now, Ma. As long as you're in your house, there's nothing they can do to you," I said, laughing. "But on a se-rious note, we didn't kill nobody. Yes, we beat Curt's ass, but that's about all. How he ended up dead is beyond me."

"Wes, the last thing I need is for you to end up back in jail for some bullshit. Donovan, you have a lot going on for yourself and this will jeopardize everything both of y'all have worked hard for. Who the fuck could've killed that boy like that?"

"Well, he was still doing his dirt in the streets, so there's no telling what happened," I said, shaking my head.

"The way they said he was gutted like a fish tells me that he pissed off a female and got caught slippin'," Dap put in his two cents.

"Shanell!" we both said at the same time.

"Why would Shanell do anything to him if she was still seeing him?" Pops asked.

"The bitch is crazy, that's why. It don't take much to set her looney ass off," Dap said, sitting down on the couch. "I'm just throwing it out there. I really don't know if she did it or not. All I know is, me and Wes didn't have shit to do with his death. We did have him leaking and bruised, but he lived to take another breath afterwards."

Justice walked in without Faith and sat down. It reminded me that she was off work early and I wanted to know why. Noticing a scratch under her eye, I walked up to her and ran my thumb over the wound.

"What happened to your face?" I asked.

She laughed and reeled her head back. "Speaking of Shanell, she showed up at my job today. I had to beat the brakes off her ass because she ran up on me. Baby, you aren't the only one that had a run in with the police. I had to tell them everything that has been going on with Shanell's ass and they locked her up."

"Man, how the fuck does she know where you work?" Dap asked.

"You know, that never crossed my mind. One of my coworkers said today wasn't the first time Shanell came into the bank. She came in looking for me in the past, but I was out on leave. Well, I'm back on leave because I was suspended today for fighting. At least I still have a job and I got to reach out and touch that bitch."

"What did they charge her with?" I asked.

"The officer said the only thing they could charge her with was assault and trespassing. When I told them about what she'd done to us, they said there's not enough evidence. Which I feel was a crock of shit, but what could I do? Arguing with them muthafuckas would've been useless."

"With those charges, she'll be out in the morning," Pops said. "Shanell needs help, for real. The way she is moving, she's not going to stop until she hurts someone. I'm going to give Bria a call and see what type of information I can get out of her about Shanell. The two of us need to have a heart to heart anyway."

"Pops, you are the best person to talk to Bria. She's not feeling any of us right now and I'm sure she wouldn't give us the time of day," Dap said as he reached for his phone. He smiled as he read what I assumed was a text before replying. "I gotta raise up out of here. The contractors are finished with Customs by Dap II and I have calls to make. It's time to promote the Grand Opening," he said proudly.

Congratulations were given along with hugs and handshakes. I was proud of my brother and couldn't wait to see him strive further in his business. He kissed my mama on her cheek and headed for the door.

"I'll keep everyone up to date because it's gonna be a party, y'all," he sang as he made his exit.

"Well, I guess that's my cue. It's time for me and my family to leave as well," I said, hugging my mama then fist bumping Pops. "Y'all don't worry about this shit they trying to pin on us. We didn't do it, and I'm not taking a hit for something I had nothing to do with."

"How about I keep Faith and the two of you go home and enjoy each other for the night?"

I looked at Justice and she cracked a smile so I knew she was down for whatever. She rose to her feet and grabbed her jacket putting it on quickly. I hugged my mama tightly and gave her another kiss on the cheek.

"Boy, get off me! Go home and enjoy your night and don't make any more babies," she said, pushing me off her.

"Thank you so much, Mama Bev. I'm looking forward to a good night's sleep." Justice hugged both of my parents and walked to the door and opened it.

"Justice, you can cancel that good night's sleep because it's not gonna happen. Make sure you stop for plenty of condoms." My mama laughed heartily.

"Bev, leave them alone. They are married and free to do whatever they want. Wes is no longer a teenager so you don't have to tell him what to do in his own home."

"Shut your mouth, Daddy. He will always be my baby and I'll tell him whatever I please and he will listen!" my mama shot back at Pops.

I left them standing in the middle of the living room going back and forth about what I was or wasn't going to do with my wife.

Slowly closing the door, I thought about all the ways I planned to caress Justice's body.

Chapter 13
Bria

Sage was sleeping soundly after he spent an hour in the tub playing with Transformers and splashing water all over my damn bathroom. I had finally finished drying up the mini pond he created and I was tired as hell. Walking down the hall to my bedroom, I climbed in my bed and immediately grabbed my laptop. There were so many orders I needed to fill as well as package up for shipping so I could take them to the post office.

Shanell had been ghost since I left her apartment. She truly pissed me off when she left my baby alone in the apartment. On top of that, she had the nerve to threaten me because she was wrong. I didn't give a damn what she had to hold over my head, I had to tell my family what the fuck was really going on.

My phone rang and I fell back on the bed because it was in the living room on the coffee table. I didn't feel like getting up to get it, so I just let it ring out. When it rang again, I groaned loudly and rolled out of the bed. By the time I made it to my phone, it had stopped ringing again. Walking slowly back to my bedroom, I lifted the phone to my face to unlock it and the ringtone blared through the speaker once again.

Pressing the green button to connect the call from my daddy, I took a deep breath before speaking. "Yes, Daddy."

"Hello, Puddin'," he said sadly into the phone.

It had been weeks since I'd talked to him and I missed him so much, but I was also still upset because he held a secret from me. My daddy was my world and nothing could ever come between us until that point. For years, I hid what I knew and tried my best not to let my feelings show. That was about to change, because I needed answers.

"Why didn't you tell me about my birth mother?" was the first thing out of my mouth. My eyes started stinging and I was on the verge of crying. When he didn't respond, it made matters worse because I felt he was going to shy away from the subject.

"Bria, I didn't think it would really matter because in my eyes, Beverly was your mother. She has been the only mother you've known and she treated you as such. You really hurt her when you said she never treated you like a daughter."

"What about how I felt? You don't think it hurt me to find out on my own that my mother wasn't my mother! That was something I should've been told when I was old enough to understand. Instead, both of you continued to hide this shit from me!"

There was no holding back my feelings. I had to let all my emotions out while I had the chance to do so and I was ready. The sound of a door closing let me know he had gone into his office to speak with me privately.

"Hear me out, baby girl. I didn't know you knew. I would've taken that secret to my grave, on some real shit. But you're right, I should've sat you down and talked to you about Rita. I didn't know how, okay? But I'm ready now if you're willing to listen," he said lowly.

"I'm listening, Daddy. I need to know about my mother."

"I wish we could talk about this face to face and not over the phone. I guess this will have to do," he said, swallowing loudly. "Rita and I met through a mutual friend at a party. We were all having a good time drinking, dancing, and just socializing. After a while, Rita was pretty drunk and was ready to go home."

He paused for a minute and continued with his story. "Rita was going to call a taxi to take her home, but I didn't have a good feeling about it so I offered to take her home. One thing led to another and I ended up sleeping with her that night. We didn't speak after that night. My homie told me Rita had been looking for me, but I wasn't trying to go there with her. I told him to give her my number the next time he saw her, but she never called.

I didn't find out about you until a week after you were born. Had she called and told me she was pregnant, I would've had to add another strike to my fuck ups with Beverly, but my responsibilities were first priority in my life."

"Hold up. So you telling me she never told you about me? How did you know to go to the hospital?" I asked.

"One of the nurses called me because Rita snuck out of the hospital and left you there. When I got to the hospital, you were hooked up to so many machines because you had many problems from Rita's drug use. Beverly stepped in as your mother the entire time you were in the NICU. Two months later, we were able to take you home and you were her baby from that day on."

Hearing my father say my mother abandoned me tugged at my heart. Knowing I wasn't wanted was a feeling I couldn't describe. Even though I had a great upbringing, I found a way to blame Beverly even though I didn't know the back story because I was jealous of my own brothers.

"Where is my mother now?" I asked. "I would like to meet her, Daddy." He didn't respond so I looked at the phone to see if the connection was lost, but it wasn't. "Daddy, are you there?" I damn near screamed.

"I'm here, baby," my daddy replied sadly. "Your mother died when you were five, Bria. She overdosed on heroin in an abandoned building. She is buried at Washington Memorial Gardens in Homewood, Illinois. I'm sorry."

Tears streamed down my face for the woman I would never get to see in person. All I thought about from the time I found out Beverly wasn't my biological mother was how I would find my mom and get to know her. That opportunity would never come for me and I didn't know how to take the news.

"Mommy, are you okay?" Sage said from the doorway.

My heart stopped because my daddy didn't know anything about my baby and in the midst of our conversation, he would find out I had a child. I held my finger to my lips for him to be quiet but whenever he saw me emotional, nothing could stop him from making sure I was alright. I put the phone on mute but it was too late. My daddy had already heard Sage in the background.

"Bria, who is that child calling you mommy?" he yelled in my ear.

Ignoring him, I stared at Sage for a moment with fresh tears running down my face. "Baby, go back to bed. I'll be in to read you a story in a few minutes. Do that for me, please," I pled to him.

"Are you okay?" he asked.

"Yes, Mommy is okay, baby. Now go," I said, trying not to chastise him harshly. Sage did as he was told and I looked down at the phone and my daddy had hung up. I breathed a sigh of relief but the phone rang and he was calling back on Facetime. Panic sat in because I didn't know how I was going to explain where I got a baby from. Instead of answering, I declined the call and sent a text.

Me: Daddy, I promise I will explain everything to you soon. This is very hard for me but give me a little time to gather my thoughts. Please don't be mad at me. There's so much that y'all don't know but I will tell you everything, I promise. I love you.

I cried harder as I sent the text to him. It took no time for him to reply back.

Daddy: Bria, what the hell do you mean you will explain soon? You need to tell me what the fuck is going on now! When did you have a baby? Why didn't I of all people know about any of this?

Me: Trust me, it's not what you think, but it's not going to sit well with you or anyone else in the family either. I'm booking a flight to come home this weekend. Gather everyone at your house once I give you my flight information. It's time for me to reveal the secret I've been hiding, but I have to do it face to face. I'm sorry, Daddy, and I hope y'all will be able to forgive me.

My daddy kept calling my phone back to back so I decided to answer because I knew if I didn't, he would be on the next thing smoking to Michigan and I couldn't have that. "Daddy, please—"

"I will give you until this weekend, Bria. But if you don't have your ass here Friday, I will be at your fuckin' door and won't nothing stop me from beating your ass! Make sure you call me with the information so I will know exactly when you will be landing."

Without waiting for a response, he hung up on me and I felt like shit. I was already in a bind with my family because I stood behind Shanell and her bullshit. Now I had to hope and pray they wouldn't disown me for the shit I was not prepared to reveal.

Chapter 14
Dap

I cruised on the expressway, bobbing my head to Nipsey Hussle's *Double Up* as I made my way to Tana's house so she could help me get these flyers ready for the Grand Opening of Custom by Dap II. I had done a radio interview to promote it earlier. A nigga was excited. Tana and I had gotten a lot closer since I introduced my dick into her life. Purposely I hadn't touched her since that day because I didn't want to base our relationship on the physical. The kitty was good as hell, but there was more to her than sex and I wanted her to fall in love with me and not with what was between my legs.

There were plenty times I was over and she tried to take things to the bedroom, but I wouldn't budge. Tana was feisty as hell and I had her spoiled from that one hit, but that shit would still be there in the future. I was a nigga that was trying to be there for the long run and not just for the time being. So, I was willing to make love to her mind and heart before I put claim on that pussy.

Tana was used to being with lame niggas. I had to make sure she could handle the real nigga I was, and that shit took time and patience. We'd been rocking for a few months and the chemistry was strong and I couldn't imagine life without her. We cooked together, chilled, and she still had me grading papers and shit, but as long as I was spending time with her, it didn't matter to me.

Pulling into the parking lot of her apartment, I got out and grabbed the bag from the passenger seat. There wasn't a day that went by that I didn't have something in hand for her. I went out and got her a dozen chocolate covered strawberries from Godiva. It was just a little something to put a smile on her face. The little shit went a long way, if you asked me. Climbing the stairs, I knocked on her door three hard times and waited patiently for her to let me in.

Tana opened the door and she was wearing a pair of boy shorts and a tank top without a bra underneath. My joint rocked up, but I screamed silently in my head at his ass. "Don't you dare react to that shit! It's a trap, nigga, calm the fuck down." I was close to licking my lips, but I checked myself and bent down and kissed her on the cheek as I placed the small bag in her hand.

"What did you buy me now?" She smiled as she looked in the bag. "Aw, these are one of my favorites. I see you really do listen when I talk to you. Thank you, Donovan. Maybe we can put some of these to use later," she smirked.

"Nah, we got all the time in the world for that shit. You'll be okay for a while longer."

"While you got me waiting, your ass is going to be competing with the motor in my vibrator whenever you decide to stop playing with me. My bitch been getting me right, so you better be ready," she laughed.

"I got that covered. You better not be stickin' that muthafucka in my gushy, I know that much. Yo' shit better clutch down on my shit like an anaconda squeezing its prey. And that's on my mama," I said, taking a seat on the couch.

Tana locked the door and walked past me with an extra swing in her hips, sitting next to me on the couch. She had drawings sprawled about the coffee table and the artwork was phenomenal. Seeing the artwork caused me to lean forward and pick one of them up.

"Damn, bae, did you draw these yourself?" I asked staring at her.

"Who else would have drawn them, Dap? Of course I drew them myself. That's what you asked me to do, right?"

"These are fuckin' amazing! I didn't think they would come out looking so professional like, that's all. You have a raw talent, Tana," I said, giving her major props. "Tell me why you aren't drawing to make money? You can sell the shit out of a painting."

"Art is a hobby for me. I love to draw, but I have to be in the mood to accomplish it. Since I've met you, I've been drawing a lot more, for some odd reason," she said, rising from the couch.

"Where are you going?" I asked, turning my head as she walked away. Her ass jiggled with every step she took and it was so cute because she didn't have much ass to jiggle. But the little bit she did have was wearing the fuck out of the shorts she wore. Tana returned with a canvas in her hand and I was curious to see what she wanted to show me.

"This was something I did from one of the pictures I took of you a while ago. I hope you like it," she said, holding the painting toward me.

Taking the painting from her hand, I turned it around slowly and my breath got caught in my throat. The image in front of me jumped out from the canvas and if I hadn't known she drew it by hand, I would've thought it was a picture that was taken with a really good camera. She caught everything from my dimples to the diamonds in my King of Customs chain. Tana even caught the dimensions of the waves in my hair. I loved the picture so much and it captured me in an exquisite light I'd never seen before.

"I love it, Tana. Thank you," I said as I stared at the detail of the portrait. "I'm going to hang this in the store and get you some clientele. This shit is too good not to be seen."

"Dap, I don't want to start drawing for people. Then it takes away from my passion, which is teaching. I can't force myself to draw on a regular basis."

"I hear what you're saying, but I'm still hanging this bad boy in the store. Would you sign it for me so I can say I have an exclusive portrait done by the infamous Montana Taylor?" I smirked.

Snatching a black Sharpie from the table, Tana held her hand out for the painting and placed it on top of the flyer samples. She scribbled her John Hancock in the bottom right corner and added a heart to the end. I was so proud of her talent and she just wasn't seeing what I saw with her skills.

"Okay, enough of that shit. Let's get down to business before it gets too late. I do have to be up early for work in the morning." She moved the canvas to the glass bar and got down to business.

"I made three different flyers and I want you to tell me which one you want to use." She handed me the flyers and sat down beside me with her laptop open. "I've set up a business page for you on several social media sites for promotional reasons. I'm not trying to hear anything about what you don't want. Word of mouth is good, but the internet is better, trust me."

I loved the way she took control and worked alongside me. Customs by Dap was a hit on the west coast, but I had to make it just as known in the Midwest. With Tana on my team, there was no way we could fail. She was showing me that she could be the brains and I definitely was the muscle of the operation.

Trying to decide which flyer I wanted to go with took well over thirty minutes. My baby didn't pressure me or anything. She continued to do whatever it was she was doing on her computer. Her fingers were moving rapidly across the keyboard and I was very impressed. She wasn't holding back with putting in work.

"What is your username and password for your website?" she asked without looking up. "As a matter of fact, just enter it for me. I have an idea."

She passed the laptop to me and I looked at it without taking it. "My username is kingcustom908 and my password is findmytrue-love, one word."

Tana looked up at me briefly before logging into my website. Scrolling her hand over the touchpad, she clicked away on the keyboard and moved her finger around constantly. After about ten minutes she turned the laptop around so I could see and I was shocked. She had made a collage of all three flyers with the portrait she had drawn in the middle on the very first page of my website.

Thousands of people browsed my site on a daily basis and for her to come up with that concept was remarkable. She made sure to include the date, time, and location of the Grand Opening as well as the color scheme. When she was done, Tana logged off my website and went back to social media and did the same using hashtags of basketball players, rappers, singers, entrepreneurs, and more so they would see my business. We had two weeks before the event and I had a feeling the turnout was going to be spectacular.

There was a knock on her door and the smile she wore turned upside down.

"Are you expecting company?" I asked.

"No. I don't know who that could be."

Whoever was at the door started banging on the door like they were the police and I jumped up, pulling my bitch off my hip. When I got to the door, I looked through the peephole and there was this peon looking light-skinned nigga with a scowl on his face on the other side of the door. Tana had a look of confusion on her face as she got up from the couch. The banging rang out again and the nigga on the other side was obviously pissed off.

"Tana, I see yo' car outside. Open this fuckin' door before I kick this bitch in!"

Tana immediately got angry and stormed over to the door. She reached out to unlock the door and I gently moved her hand and shook my head. Placing my gun behind my back, I made up my mind that this fool wasn't worth wasting a bullet on. Unlocking the door, I opened it and leaned against it with a smirk on my face.

"Who the fuck is you?"

"Yo' worse muthafuckin' nightmare if you don't get the fuck away from this apartment," I gritted.

"Man, where is Tana? I'm her nigga and you shouldn't even be here!"

I laughed in his fuckin' face because he was acting like a bitch nigga. "You her man, but you trying to get inside the spot I'm already in. Brah, I'm trying to be nice about this shit right now, but you pushin' me to a point of no return."

He tried to push his way into the apartment, but he had nothing on my 6'3", one hundred ninety-five pound frame. I didn't budge, but I did reach out, clasp my hand around his throat, drag his ass inside, and closed the door. He got his wish of coming in, but he wasn't going to like the outcome.

"There she is. What do you want to say to her?" I growled.

"Ack. Ack," was the only thing he could force out of his mouth. My thumb was pressed against his throat and I shoved him backwards with force. His head banged against the wall with a thud.

"Speak yo' piece, nigga! You wanted to talk to her. Do that shit so you can get the fuck outta here!" I barked.

He rubbed his neck and coughed a couple times before turning to Tana. "I love you, Tana. Why you not trying to work this out?" he asked softly.

"Aht, aht, nigga. What happened to your outside voice? You know, the one you were using when you were on the other side of that door?"

"Who the fuck is you?" he yelled at me.

"Her man, nigga! That's the reason yo' advances are being ignored. I don't know what the fuck you did, but you let a real nigga step in. You don't have a chance in hell of getting back in with Tana. She's off the market."

Tana stepped forward to put a stop to the back and forth that was going on between me and the lame. She placed a hand on my chest and smiled as she stared into my eyes. The lame's nose flared and he took a step toward her and I was ready to react. Before I could, Tana reached up and pulled my head down and planted a kiss on my chin.

"It's okay," she said, palming my face. Pivoting in the lame's direction, she pointed her finger at him. "Tyson, we've been through this shit countless times, so don't think I'm putting on a show because Dap is present."

My head jerked because Tana called me by my street name. But I had to let that shit slide because Donovan was just as lame as Tyson in my book. So Dap it was, and I poked my chest out a little bit.

"When you left me, I told you there was no coming back. I meant that shit, Tyson. It's been months since you decided to move on with someone else, and I let you have that. Bothering you wasn't on my agenda. Calling you repeatedly wasn't part of my plan either. I just let you go. But in the process, someone found me and is appreciating the woman you took for granted."

Tana looked up at me and grabbed my hand, squeezing it lightly. "I'm happy. Make this your last time coming to my home. As I told you before, I won't change my number, nor will I block you. Just do what's right and leave me the fuck alone. That's all I want from you."

"Bitch, you must be out yo' mind if you think I'm about to allow you to be with another nigga!" he said, grabbing her by the back of her neck like she was a baby pitbull.

Before he could get a nice grip on her, he was Wilder and I was Fury all over his ass. Tana was trying to pull me off him by the back of my shirt, but I was fuckin' his ass all the way up. My fist connected with his front tooth and I felt the skin break on my knuckles. None of that stopped me though because I was in a zone of my own.

His punk ass balled up on the floor covering his face as I stood over him, delivering punch after punch to his head. "Nigga, you outta pocket for putting yo' muthafuckin' hands on what's mine!" I said, delivering a punch to his ribcage. "The only bitch I see in this muthafucka is you!"

Tana threw her body in front of me and I had to pull my fist back so I wouldn't punch her ass. When I looked down at Tyson's punk ass, he had blood dripping from his mouth, eye, and nose. His shirt had a trail of blood on it too, but I didn't give a damn.

"Dap! That's enough, okay? He's not worth it. I promise you, he's not worth it."

Tyson took that moment to jump up as fast as he could and bolted out the door. I wanted to follow him and fuck him up some more, but I didn't want to bring any heat to Tana's spot. It was bad enough he was banging on the door like he didn't have no fuckin' sense. Tana closed the door and rested her back against it with her eyes closed.

"I'm sorry. I swear I broke things off with him—"

"You don't have to explain nothing. I already know what the fuck he's on. The next time he comes around, I'm putting a bullet in his shit. He's only breathing because you asked me to stop. His ass could've died tonight but on the strength of you, he lives to see another day. He won't be lucky the next time."

Tana grabbed my hand and looked at my hand. "Let's go clean you up, champ." She laughed. "I had to throw in the towel so you wouldn't have his ass in here looking like Wilder."

Meesha

"That's crazy that you said that shit because I was thinking the same thing as I was beating his ass." I laughed as she led me to the bathroom.

Chapter 15
Shanell

I was in lockup for two days before someone came back to the holding cell to set me free. The bench I was lying on had my back stiff as a board, I was funky as hell, and my mouth felt as if I drank Elmer's glue for breakfast; pasty as hell. Someone stood by the bars silently, but I knew someone was there. Removing my hand from over my eyes, I turned my head to see who was being a creep. Officer Johnson stood outside the bars with a sour expression displayed on his face. It was a clear indication he wasn't pleased with the fact he had nothing to hold me on.

"You're free to go, Miss Jones," he said dryly as he unlocked the cell door. "If I hear your name in this precinct or even see your name pop up in the system with any association with the Kings, I'm coming to lock your ass up personally."

Placing my feet on the floor, I rubbed my eyes and glared at him. "Save that jibber jabber for the day you come to lock me up then. For now, I'm out of here. Lead me to the process of walking out of this dirty ass place."

I stood up as he opened the door and waited for him to state a command. Officer Roman gripped my arm firmly and led me away from the cell.

It took over an hour to process me out of the jail. When I walked out of the station, I pulled my phone out of my purse and it was dead as a doorknob. Digging through my purse, I checked to see how much cash I had and there was enough for me to flag down a taxi.

It didn't take long for a taxi to stop for me. I jumped in and gave him directions to the location where I'd left my car. Ten minutes later I was walking to my car that had been parked for the past two days. There were three tickets on my car and I was pissed. Without looking at the tickets, I unlocked the driver's door and hopped inside.

Immediately connecting my phone to the charger, I turned the key in the ignition and merged into traffic. As I drove through the downtown streets of Chicago, many thoughts of revenge entered my mind. Justice had put herself at the top of my list along with her husband. Both of them were going to feel my wrath.

There were so many malicious thoughts running through my mind, but I didn't want to concentrate on that at the moment. I hit the power button on the radio, the DJ's voice blared through the speakers. Barely listening to what he was saying, I drove up the entrance ramp of the expressway and pushed the gas pedal.

"Y'all don't forget about the big event that's going down, Friday March 13ᵗʰ. Our very own Donovan "Dap" King is having a Grand Opening for his Customs by Dap II location downtown on Michigan Avenue. King's custom store in California is booming and he is bringing that heat to the Chi. We have to rep our own so, get ready, because it's about to be lit! The party is going down at Lady Loves Nightclub. There will be door prizes, food, drinks, and music by yours truly, DJ Spin! You will want to be in the building!"

"This muthafucka doing the damn thing, I see," I said to myself. "I got something for your ass too, Dap." I laughed loudly as Jhené Aiko's "Triggered" started playing.

> *Go figure*
> *You were the trigger*
> *You brought me to an obstructed view*
> *When you knew the picture was bigger*
> *Who am I kidding?*
> *Knew from the beginning*
> *You'd ruin everything, you do it every time*
> *You are my enemy, you are no friend of mine, mu'fucka*

As the song played, my thoughts went wild and I smiled as I listened to the lyrics. "Damn, I'm 'bout to burn this bitch down," I sang along with Jhené.

I knew exactly what I had to do, and the scenario played in my head as I signaled to get off at my exit. After turning down my street, I parked in front of my apartment building and threw the car in park. As I got out of my car, a chick that I'd only seen in passing was coming out of the building.

"Hey, girl. I haven't seen you in a while," she said, smiling.

I didn't know her ugly ass, but she was trying to act like she was one of the homies or some shit. I came home to mind my own business. There was no reason anyone should be clocking my moves. It was clear indication the bitch was about to be nosy as fuck and I was ready to read her ass like a book.

"Do you know me?" I asked, climbing the stairs.

"Not per se, but we are neighbors and I live next door from you. I'm Jasmine, by the way," she said, holding her hand out and smiling.

Looking down at her hand, I brought my eyes back up to her face and ignored the polite gesture of shaking her hand. "Well, that's good to hear, but I don't need any friends around here. I don't know y'all and I want to keep it that way," I said, walking past her into the building.

"Just so you know, some detectives came by here knocking on your door," she yelled out behind me. "They slid a card under your door and they might come back. I'm giving you a heads up and you want to be nasty. Enjoy the rest of your day."

By the time I turned around, she had walked away, but I could tell she was big mad.

When I unlocked the door to my apartment, there was indeed a business card on the floor when I stepped inside. I closed and locked my door before bending down to retrieve the card. The name on the top read "Detective Roman" with a number to reach him.

Why is a detective coming to my damn house? I haven't done shit that warrants them to come for me, I thought to myself.

"Bitch, we gave that nigga a cesarean!" the voice in my head laughed evilly. "Yo' ass know why they're looking for you, but you better play the muthafuckin' part because I'm not trying to be locked in a six by eight jail cell."

"Shut the fuck up!" I screamed, storming to my bedroom.

Throwing the card on the dresser as I entered my room, I snatched my shirt over my head and my pants followed. As soon as

I got the chance, I was going to burn that shit in the nearest alley. I opened the top drawer of my dresser and grabbed a pair of leggings and a T-shirt before walking down the hall to the bathroom. I turned the knob in the shower, stepped in the tub, and let the water beat down on me.

It felt good to wash the funk off my body since I hadn't had a shower in over forty-eight hours. As I reached for the shea butter body wash and my loofah, the voice in my head started humming. I hadn't been out of jail for a solid two hours and the bitch was prompting me to cause hell once again. The thought of taking my meds was strong, but I had flushed them muthafuckas months prior and the only way to get more was to go see my psychiatrist, and that wasn't happening.

"Born to fight, trained to kill, ready to die, but we never will," the voice in my head sang.

"We have to give it time! Shit is hot, now leave me the fuck alone!"

"Time? Bitch, these muthafuckas take you for a joke! Time will only give them the opportunity to come for your head. Don't be stupid and let that li'l pussy steer you in the wrong direction. We killed Curt. Who do you think will caress your walls now? Sure as hell not Wes! You have to shed blood to get that orgasm now," the voice laughed.

Covering my ears, I stepped under the water to drown out the words of my inner self. After about ten minutes, I came out and everything was silent. I scrubbed my body a couple times and shut the water off before grabbing a towel and wrapping it around my body. I walked back to my room with clothes in hand and my phone was ringing from my purse in the living room. By the time I reached my purse, it stopped.

I fumbled through my purse until I found my phone. The name on the display shook me a little bit. I slowly walked back to my room as I stared down at the missed call from Curt's phone. There was no way his ass survived my deadly attack. As I stepped through the doorway, the phone started ringing in my hand. Once again, it was the ghost of Curt's past, but being the crazy bitch I was, I answered without hesitation.

"Hey, bae," I said into the phone. The person on the other end didn't reply and I wasn't in the mood to play games. "Curt, what the hell you doing? I know you didn't call to breathe in the phone."

"Who the fuck is this?" a female asked.

"Nah, you called me, so you obviously know who the fuck I am," I shot back.

"That's where you're wrong. The name under this number is Cum Sucker. Is that you?" she asked snidely.

"That's an accurate description, so yes," I laughed. "What can I help you with?"

"Bitch, what was your relationship with my man?"

I had to pause because she was dumb as fuck calling me about a dead nigga. It had to be his baby mama, and the bitch was fishing hard to get the inside scoop. What she didn't understand about me was that I had the tea that would fuck up her respiratory system.

"Correction, boo. Don't you mean what's my situationship with your man? What me and Curt have is far from a relationship. That's where you come in at," I laughed. "But to answer your question, he was the nigga that enjoyed coming over to eat out my ass and left after paying. Anything else?"

Baby mama was stuck and didn't know what to say after my rebuttal. But that should teach her ass not to ask questions she wasn't ready for in the future. I had no problem making a bitch shed a couple tears over their good for nothing ass nigga. It wasn't my job to keep it cute for no muthafuckin' body.

"Did you know he had a woman?" she asked stupidly.

"Bitch, where's Curt? He is the one you should be questioning, not me. I don't lay down with you every night."

"Curt is dead!" she cried out. "I just collected his belongings and was going through his phone. Bitches like you make it hard for bitches like me."

"Blah, blah, blah. If the nigga is dead, why is it important for you to contact me? That nigga is doing a gangsta praise dance with the Lord and you're pressed about what he was doing while he was breathing. Miss me with that goofy shit and cry on your own time."

I hung up on her ass because there was nothing Curtis Miles could do for me from the grave. His bitch should concentrate on grieving and leave me the fuck out of her bullshit. Tossing the phone on my bed, I sat down and rubbed lotion over my body before slipping on my clothes.

"Shanell, you need to disable that bitch!" the voice in my head screamed. "She was out of line for calling you."

"I'm not killing that girl! Don't start with me, okay?"

"You better do something because I have an urge that's building by the minute. I'm trying to give you the opportunity to get shit moving on your own. There will be nothing you can do if you keep procrastinating. I'm nothing to play with when you can't control what I do without you."

"All I have to do is take my meds and you will go away! Then what would you be saying?"

"Bitch, I'll knock all that shit on the floor and cause yo' looney ass to kill yo'self. Don't fuck with me, Shanell, you won't win. But I'll leave you alone until you can't handle this shit on your own."

"Fuck you!" I screamed loudly.

There was no response, so I knew my inner self had vanished. I was going to be locked up for life if I let things go according to her plan.

Chapter 16
Dap

Tana and I were getting the grand opening together nicely. Without her, I don't know how I would've made it through the ordeal. The radio advertisement was airing and I got excited every time I heard it. Business was booming online and in Cali and I was grateful for it all.

I'd just left the last meeting with the party planner. I decided to make the event kind of like an all-black affair, but the color scheme would be black and maroon. I couldn't wait to get fresh and see Tana on her grown woman, elegant shit.

While at my meeting, I received a call from my father. He wanted me to come to his house at two o'clock. It was Saturday and I was tired as hell, but when Wes Sr. called, something was up. It was a little after one and I didn't see any reason to prolong going that way.

I was thinking about what could be so urgent that he wanted me to come over on such short notice. "Hey Siri," I said after pressing the button on my phone. "Call Wes."

"Okay, I'm on it," Siri replied. "Calling Wes." Signaling to get from behind a slow driver, I waited for Wes to answer his phone.

"What's up, bro?" he asked into the phone.

"Man, I'm on my way to Pops' crib. Did he call you too?" I asked.

"Yeah. I called his ass and asked what was going on, and all he said was, just be there. I can't even call it, bro. Me, Justice, and Faith is heading out in a few, so I guess I'll see you when I get there."

"Aight. This shit has been on my mind since I received the call. Luckily I was already out or a nigga would be asleep."

"What the hell had you up and about early on a Saturday?" he asked.

"I had to meet up with the party planner for the grand opening. We're gonna have to go shopping for this one, bro."

"I'm ready. That advertisement on the radio is a hit!" he said excitedly.

"That was Tana's idea. Man, that woman has pulled all this shit together like a champ. I'm grateful to have her on my team. She's definitely going on the payroll," I said proudly. "Speaking of Tana, I haven't talked to you, but I had to beat the fuck outta her ex the other day."

"I heard," he laughed. "She called Justice and told her all about it. I was waiting on you to hit me up. How's your hand?"

"Man, you know that shit was nothing. I got hands of steel, and hopefully the nigga learned what not to do when it comes to me. He fucked up puttin' his hands on her and calling her a bitch. It was over for his ass after that. Nigga would've died had she not got in front of him, stopping me from beating his muthafuckin' head in."

"I don't understand why niggas don't understand when I woman says it's over, it's over. Leave her the fuck alone."

"Wes, are you ready?" Justice asked in the background.

"Yeah, baby," he replied back to her. "Aye, bro, I'll see you at Pops' shortly. Don't be out there fuckin' nobody up. Your fighting days are over. It's time to get this money."

"I hear ya. But you know I'll put these paws on a nigga expeditiously with no hesitations. Drive carefully. I'm out," I said, pushing the button to end the call.

It took maybe fifteen minutes after talking to Wes for me to get to my father's crib. Pulling up, I parked on the street so when it was time for me to bail out, I didn't have to wait for anyone to move their car. As I got out of the car, my phone chimed with a text.

Juice: Aye, Dap man. You need to hit me up asap, my nigga. Shit is fucked up in Cali.

I immediately hit Juice's name in my call log. It didn't take long for him to answer. "That was fast," he said quickly.

"What's going on, Juice?" I asked.

"Man, it's all on the news here. Rocco was found dead last night in his crib. The reporter said he was shot five times in his doorway. They are saying it was a hit."

The words Juice said took the wind out of me because the last thing I was expecting him to say was that my mentor was gone. I had just talked to him about the grand opening days prior and he said he would be in the building. The shit broke a nigga's heart because Rocco was like a father to me and to hear that he was gone did something to my mental.

"You still there, man?"

"Yeah, I'm here. What is the word on the street? Is anybody saying anything?" I asked, trying to fight back the tears that stung the back of my eyes.

"Rocco came into Customs just yesterday while I was there. At first, he said he was checking to see how things were going at the store, then he motioned for me to come outside with him," Juice paused.

"What did he say, Juice?" I asked anxiously.

"If you'd let me finish, I'll tell you!" he snapped. "Rocco seemed kind of spooked, to be honest, fam. He demanded for me to beef up security at Customs because he had a feeling something was going to go down. I'm not in charge of Customs, but I put some of my best shooters on the job. You've always believed in me and I owe you my life."

"Thanks, fam. You don't owe me shit, believe that. I knew what I was doing when I left you in charge. You're doing just what I would've done in your position. Keep ya eyes open. I have a few calls to make and I'll get back with you soon as I get some insight on what happened."

"Sounds good and I'm sorry about Rocco, Dap. I know how much he meant to you, and I'll see what I can find out this way," Juice said sincerely. "On a happier note, I've heard your advertisement all the way on the west coast, nigga! Customs II is going to blow the fuck up! I'll be there to support. Get ready because we're bringing Cali to the Chi and we're coming hard!"

"That's what's up, Juice." The excitement wasn't the same coming from me, but I knew when the time came, we were going to turn up.

Meesha

"Keep ya head up, Boss. We're going to get through this shit. Handle your business and I'll be waiting on your call. Peace."

Juice ended the call and as I was about to call Christian, Rocco's brother, the door to the house opened and Beverly stepped out on the porch. She looked more like a big sister than a mother. The grey at her temples was the only indication of her being older than she appeared.

"What are you doing out here? I've watched you pace back and forth for damn near ten minutes on your phone."

Hitting the button on my key fob, I slowly walked toward the house with a lot going on in my mind. My heart was heavy and I was struggling to hide the emotions I was feeling inside. When I made it to the top of the stairs, I fell into Beverly's outstretched arms.

"What's the matter, baby?" she asked, rubbing my back.

I felt like a punk crying like a child. I rarely showed my emotions for others to see. Beverly gave me time to get out one last cry before she pushed me back slightly and I automatically lowered my head.

"Talk to me, Donovan," Beverly said as I attempted to turn away from her. She clutched my forearm firmly. "Don't shut me out. It's been a long time since I've seen you this way."

Wiping my eyes, I faced her and faked a smile. "I'm okay," I sniffed. "I just got a call I wasn't prepared for. Do you remember Rocco? The man that helped me take Customs to the next level?" I asked.

"Yeah, what about him?"

"He was killed last night. I don't know the details, but this shit hurts, Bev. He was like a second father to me," I said, tearing up again. "I believe whoever killed him is coming after Customs. I'm not a hunnid percent sure, but I have to be ready for whatever," I explained.

"Why would someone come for you behind Rocco? I don't understand."

"Rocco passed his business to me and not his sons. He said they weren't capable of running his business and they didn't like being

118

left out. I'm not saying his sons had anything to do with his death, but they are on the top of my list." My cell phone chimed and I looked down at the text I'd received.

(213)555-0523: When you cut off the head, the body will fall. You going down, motherfucker. Guardati le spalle (watch your back)

I stared at the message for a bit too long. Beverly inched over and peered over my shoulder, but I stuffed the phone in my pocket before she could see anything. I glanced in her direction. "Where's Pops?" I asked, trying to take the attention off the shit that was brewing with me.

"He should be on his way back. Come on inside," she said, walking toward the house. Wes' car turned into the driveway causing Beverly to swivel back around. "There goes Granny's baby," she said happily.

"Bev, why do Pops want us here?" I asked as we watched Wes get out of the car.

"You will find out when he gets here. He doesn't want me to say anything. But it is necessary for everyone to be here," she responded. "Hey y'all! Bring my baby to me."

"What about me?" Wes's spoiled ass threw over his shoulder as he took Faith out of the backseat.

"Baby, leave the whining to Faith please. You are no longer your mother's favorite." Justice laughed as she climbed the stairs, giving Beverly a tight hug. "How are you, Mama Beverly?"

"I'm good now that my baby is here." Beverly smiled. "You're looking good, Justice. It doesn't look like you had a baby months ago."

"I got that snapback. What can I say?" Justice laughed.

"Why are we here?" Wes asked. "I could be laid up right now."

"Everybody, come inside. Your father should be back any moment and he will explain this meeting. As I've told Donovan, I was told not to discuss the matter," Beverly said, leading the way into the house.

I sat on the loveseat and my phone vibrated again. Taking a deep breath, I pulled my phone out of my pocket. There was a text from Tana and it made me smile.

Tana: Good afternoon. I just want you to know I'm proud of you and I can't wait to see your name being mentioned by many. Get ready because you're about to blow up! Enjoy the rest of your day.

As I was about to respond to Tana's text, another came through. I exited out of the current one and open the new text.

(213) 555-0523: You are a dead man walking. Rocco is gone and you are next LOL

"Brah, you good over there?" Wes asked.

"Yeah," I said, standing to my feet. "I'm going out back to make a call. I'll be right back. Let me know when Dad gets here," I said, going out of the back door.

Quickly dialing Christian's number, I waited anxiously for him to pick up. When he didn't answer, I thought the worst as I redialed the number. Holding my breath with every ring, I finally let it out when he answered.

"Ciao, Dap," Christian said solemnly.

"What happened, Christian? Who did this?"

"The shit is sad, to be honest. Rocco loved them boys and this is how they repay him!" Christian yelled. "How do you shoot your father five times? Once in the face!" he cried. "My brother didn't deserve to die like that!"

"Are you saying that Arturro and Luciano did this?" I asked, stunned.

"That's exactly what I'm saying! They killed him for money, Dap. Rocco would give them anything they needed, but both of them were greedy. They blew through money and expected Rocco to continue to dish out cash when they wanted it. The insurance money will set them straight for the rest of their lives."

My mouth was damn near on the floor listening to Christian speak. The hurt in his voice pulled at my heartstrings and I knew just how he felt because I was in the same boat. The conversation I had with Rocco came to mind and it replayed repeatedly in my head.

"Don't worry, everything is alright." That was the only thing I heard. But it was not alright because Rocco was no longer here on earth.

"You still there, Buddy?" Christian asked.

"Yeah. How deep is this shit, Unc?" I needed to know so I'd be ready when or if Rocco's sons came for me.

"The situation wasn't deep for my brother at all. He was adamant about what he wanted to do, and he did it. Arturro and Luciano took things too far because of bitterness. You should be receiving a package in the mail in a couple of days, but I'm going to fill you in on the contents of the package." I sat waiting for Christian to continue because I was curious to hear where this was going.

"Rocco put many things in place months ago, Dap. He changed his will." Christian paused. "He took his sons completely off and added you as sole beneficiary of his estate. Arturro and Luciano were left with one hundred thousand dollars apiece, which neither knows about at this time. They are going to come for you, Dap. I'm working hard on my end to find them."

"Christian, why would Rocco do that? If he didn't want his sons to have it, why not give it to you?" I asked.

"I worked with my brother from the time he started his business over thirty years ago. I'm just as wealthy as he was. Rocco knew I would reject his offer to take over his estate. We agreed that you were the best person to carry on his legacy. As we speak, Donovan King, you are now a billionaire, my friend."

I fell to my knees and almost dropped my phone. All my life I'd always said I would be a millionaire. Now here I was a billionaire and I didn't want any parts of it. Losing Rocco, to me, wasn't worth the money. There was no way I could enjoy the luxury handed to me without him being by my side.

"Christian, I can't accept that," I said honestly.

"You can and you will! It's already done and you will receive the paperwork in the mail. There are other things Rocco sent as well. I will be here for you when needed. As a matter of fact, I will be at your grand opening, as your security team. It's what Rocco wanted. Do not come back to California. There won't be a funeral because my brother wanted to be cremated."

"I have already received a couple of threatening text messages. They came from this number," I said scrolling through my text messages. "(213)-555-0523. Do you know whose number that is?" I asked.

"That's Luciano's number. You will be seeing me before your grand opening. The police have been looking for both Luciano and Arturro since last night. They may be on their way to you. Be careful out there, Dap. I'll see you soon once I tie up things around here. Ciao."

I ended the call and sat on the chair closest to the door and put my head in my hands. This shit was about to take me back to the street life and it wasn't the time for all of that bullshit. But I stayed ready, so anybody could get it if they came for me.

Chapter 16
Bria

I was nervous as fuck stepping off the plane at Midway Airport. Sage was excited because he loved getting on the plane. I didn't know how my father was going to react to seeing my baby in the flesh, but he definitely was going to be pissed. Prolonging my trip for a day probably wasn't the right thing to do, but I wasn't ready to face my family about Sage. I had damn near six years of explaining to do, and I didn't know where to begin. As I walked to luggage claim to retrieve our bags, I got a call from my daddy.

"We just landed," I said without saying hello. "I'm on my way to baggage claim now and then I'll be out."

"Okay, I'll be outside waiting for you," he said, hanging up.

Sage had his nose in that damn tablet and was walking slow as hell. I snatched the gadget from his hand and pulled him along so we could get to baggage claim. He started whining and I hated when he did that shit. I stopped in the middle of the floor, forcing people to walk around us, and bent down to his level.

"Cut that out now, Sage! You're not paying attention and we need to get out of this airport," I spoke to him sternly. "I don't have time for your bratty ways right now. You will hold my hand and not let it go. Is that understood?"

He shook his head yes and I hated that shit too because he could talk any other time, but now he wanted to use head motions. Nah, I wasn't going for that shit. "Don't you know how to talk? Answer me, Sage. Do you understand me?"

"Yes, Mommy, I understand but you are being really mean to me," he said as tears rolled down his face.

I felt like shit because I didn't realize I was taking my frustrations out on him. Shit was about to get real with my family and I didn't know what to do. I didn't know how to tell them what needed to be said. Shit, I was scared as hell.

"I'm sorry, baby. Mommy wasn't purposely being mean. Come on so we can get our luggage and get out of here, okay?"

"Okay, Mommy. I'm ready," Sage said, wiping his eyes with the back of his hand.

When we got to baggage claim, I immediately saw our bags and grabbed them before they rolled around again. I gave Sage his custom blue luggage that had his name stitched in big black letters. He raised the handle and was ready to go. Doing the same with mine, I then placed his tablet in his backpack before grabbing his hand, heading for the exit.

I made sure Sage was bundled up before we walked out of the door and spotted my daddy parked right outside the doors with his hazard lights flashing. He got out of the car after popping the trunk and stared at Sage and smiled. My baby looked up at me, then back at my daddy as he snuggled closer to me.

"Hey, lil man," my daddy said, kneeling down in front of Sage. "I'm your grandpa. What's your name?"

Sage hesitated before responding. "Sage Xander King."

"That's my name too! You have the name of a warrior. Did you know that?"

Sage shook his head no and hugged my leg tighter. I pried his arm from around my leg and led him to the car. Taking his luggage from him, I opened the back door and took the backpack from Sage's back so he could climb inside.

"Put your seat belt on," I said, watching him move swiftly to complete the task. I handed him his backpack and he immediately took out that damn tablet.

My daddy took both bags from the curb and placed them in the trunk. He walked back as I closed the door and stared at me, shaking his head. Disappointment was evident on his face and I couldn't find any words to say. Bypassing me, my daddy opened the passenger door and I slowly got inside and waited for him to close the door.

When he was seated in the driver's seat, he glanced in the rearview mirror at Sage before turning off the hazards and signaling to pull into traffic. The first ten minutes of the ride was quiet and made me wonder what my daddy was thinking. I glanced in his direction and his jaw was clenched tightly. I knew he had a lot to say, but didn't want to do so in the presence of Sage.

"Sage, put your headphones on, baby," I said over my shoulder.

"Okay, sorry Mommy."

Once he had his headphones in place, I turned to my daddy. "Say what you have to say. I know it's a shock for you to find out I have a child this way."

"Bria, how old is Sage?" he asked without taking his eyes off the road.

"He will be six, May 17th," I replied lowly.

"Six! Bria, you have been home countless times and you have never even mentioned this child. Do you know how much time has passed and Sage don't know shit about his family?" my daddy yelled glancing back at Sage.

"I know and I'm sorry. I—"

"You're sorry? Where have you been hiding him all these years? I've come to Michigan to visit and there were no signs of a child in your home! Why did you feel you needed to keep this from us? Fuck that, from me! We talked often up until the bullshit you pulled at Justice and Wes' baby shower. You have a lot of explaining to do."

"It wasn't my intention to keep him hidden. I just didn't know how to tell you I had a baby," I said, looking away from him.

"Bria, we talk about everything! Why did you think you couldn't talk to me about this? I would never turn my back on you because you got pregnant. Is this the reason you up and moved?"

"It was part of the reason," I replied. "I just had to leave, okay?"

"Where is his father, Bria?" my daddy asked, stopping at a red light.

"I don't know where he is. Sage is being taken care of by me, his mother. I don't need his father to do anything for him. I got this."

"Who is this muthafucka? Wait, do this nigga even know he has a damn son?" my daddy asked in a steely tone.

"No," I whispered.

"What was that?" he asked, driving through the intersection.

"No. He doesn't know and no I don't want him to know," I said nervously. "I don't want to talk about him. He's irrelevant. All I want to do is introduce Sage to the family so there won't be any more secrets. Like you said, it's been too long and too many years have already passed."

"Bria, this shit is a hard pill to swallow. I feel there is more to all of this, but I will allow you to tell me the whole truth whenever you're ready. Sage is my grandson and I will be there for him from this point on. Don't ever in your life keep something of this magnitude from me again."

"There is more to it, Daddy, but I don't want to go into it at this time. I'll be here until tomorrow afternoon and you can spend as much time as you want with Sage. That's why we're here," I said, telling half the truth.

"I'm telling you now, this shit may not go over so smoothly with your mother—"

"She's not my mother," I said snidely.

"Don't start that bullshit! You and Beverly will sit down and have a discussion because she doesn't deserve the attitude you have towards her. She is the only mother you know and if you want to be mad at anyone, it should be me. As a matter of fact, why aren't you mad at me? Let's talk about that shit."

"I have no reason to be mad at you, Daddy. You have always been there for me."

"Bev's been there for you just as much as me! I should be the one you're mad at because it was my dick that produced yo' ass! Beverly only did what I asked of her, and that was to be the best mother she could be for you. She treated you like her own because she is my wife! She could've left my ass to be a single father and I don't know what type of child you would've turned out to be in the process."

Tears stung the back of my eyes because he was right. Beverly never mistreated me, but when I found out she wasn't my biological mother, the resentment grew every time I thought about the truth that was never shared with me. It was like I lived my whole life as a lie. I felt like I didn't know who I truly was, and that caused me to develop hate for my brothers. Helping Shanell only gave me reason to hurt the ones that had nothing but love for me.

126

We weren't too far from the house when my phone rang. I took it from my purse and saw it was Shanell calling. I declined the call because I truly didn't want to talk to her. Putting the phone on silent, I pushed it back down in my purse.

When my daddy turned onto his street, my heart started beating fast because there were extra cars in the driveway and parked in front of the house.

"What made you give Sage my middle name?" my daddy asked, pulling into the driveway.

"I didn't want him to have your full name, so I gave him your middle name instead," I said, turning around to look at my baby. Sage was knocked out with a little spittle running from his mouth. "He is out cold," I said out loud. Unbuckling the seatbelt, I reached out and removed the headphones from his head. He didn't move an inch, but when I attempted to take the tablet from his hand, he clutched it like a white woman walking past a black man.

"Come on, baby. We're at Grandpa's house," I laughed.

Sage sat up, looking around as he wiped his mouth. I opened the passenger door and got out. My daddy had stepped out as well and walked around to the back door. As soon as he opened it, Sage was ready to start that running shit.

"Don't you dare," I said, giving him the look I saw often growing up.

"I wasn't going to run, Mommy."

"Yeah, okay," I said, closing the door. Sage stood waiting for me patiently.

"I'm glad you learned something from me. That stare was amazing." My daddy laughed as he whispered in my ear. "Let's go, Sage. There's plenty of people inside that's going to be shocked to meet you," he said, reaching out for Sage's hand.

"Okay, but do you know my daddy?" Sage asked.

"No, I don't know your daddy, but you're about to meet two of the coolest uncles in the world. Are you ready?"

"Yeah, I'm ready. Just let them know they can't be cooler than me," he said, skipping alongside my daddy as they headed for the house.

I slowly walked behind them because I still wasn't ready to face my family as far as Sage was concerned. My daddy and Sage waited until I climbed the stairs before opening the door. I could hear people talking from the living room as I closed the door behind me. The chatter came to a halt the minute Sage entered the room holding my father's hand.

"Weston Sr., I know damn well you haven't brought another damn kid in this house for me to raise!" Beverly yelled angrily. "I thought you were going to the fuckin' airport to pick up Bria!"

"Bev, shut all that shit up, would you? I did go get Bria. This is her son Sage," he said, removing the hat from Sage's head.

"Bria's son?" Wes asked as he stared at Sage. "When were you pregnant?" he added, standing to his feet.

"That's what the fuck I'm trying to figure out," Dap chimed in. "I was only in Cali four years and you were already gone to Michigan. When did this shit happen?"

I stepped deeper into the room and bent down to take Sage's coat off. "Would y'all save that for later and just get to know him, please?"

"Nah, that's not gon' work with me," Dap said, walking forward. "Hey, bae. Take li'l man upstairs for a few minutes while we holla at Bria."

The bitch that was talking shit at the baby shower stepped forward and reached out for Sage. I wanted to swing on her ass, but it wasn't the time for the bullshit. She only did what the fuck she was supposed to do as a friend. Nodding my head, I handed my baby his tablet before he followed the bitch upstairs. It was about to be an interrogation of a lifetime for me.

Chapter 17
Wes

Once Tana and Sage were out of earshot, I stood in front of my sister with my arms folded over my chest. Bria stood chewing on her bottom lip, and that was a clear indication she was nervous. Both of my parents used to get on her about it because she would chew until she drew blood.

"Stop chewing on your lip," every one of us said at the same time. That caused us to laugh, breaking the ice just a tad bit, but Bria wasn't getting off that easily.

"What's shorty's name, Bria?" I asked, spreading my feet apart.

"Sage. His name is Sage."

"Who is his daddy?" I shot back at her quickly.

She looked at me and frowned before responding. "You wouldn't know him if I gave you a name. All that matters is, he's your nephew. Anything else is irrelevant."

"Shid, bro, that lil nigga looks like yo' ass," Dap said, laughing. "If anything, his little ass should look like Pop, not your ass."

Justice's eyes furrowed and Beverly gave me a questioning look as well. I didn't want them to start speculating about shit. Dap's ass was taking this shit into another direction just to start something with his petty ass.

"Man, that boy don't look like me! And if there's a resemblance, that's because his mama is my damn sister." I laughed too.

Beverly stood up and walked to the staircase. "Tana, bring that baby down here!" she yelled upstairs.

A couple minutes, later Tana and Sage were coming down to join the rest of us. I was focusing on Sage's face the entire time and when he looked up, my heart skipped a beat. Dap was right, he did look identical to me as a kid. Walking toward Sage, I bent down to his level and he had the nerve to grill my ass.

"Why do everybody keep getting in my face? That's rude you know," Sage said.

"Chill out, lil homie. I just want to introduce myself to you. I'm your uncle Wes," I said, holding out my hand for him to shake.

"It's good to meet you. I've never had an uncle before. But I learned never to shake anybody's hand after I saw this kid named Tommy at my school scratch his balls and touch somebody." Instead, Sage held his fist towards me so I could bump it.

I laughed so hard I fell over. Sage even talked like me and had a sense of humor out of this world. Dap walked over and kneeled down in front of Sage and he was trying his best not to laugh along with me.

"What's up, Sage? I'm your uncle Donovan," he introduced himself, holding out his fist. "Now you have two uncles that you can tell your friends about when you go back home. Tell me a little bit about yourself, nephew."

"Well, I'm five going on six. I'm in kindergarten and I get all A's on my report card. I've been student of the month the whole school year, and those other kids don't got nothing on my swag. Oh, and I'm the only kid in my class with a girlfriend. Her name is Olivia. Do you know my daddy? Because I think Olivia's daddy is going to be a problem?"

Both me and Dap were laughing our asses off at the shit he said about Olivia's daddy. This kid was a character and I loved it. Glancing over at Bria, I saw that she had sat down in the chair close to the window. Dap had his head down, but when he lifted it back up, he had tears running down his face.

"Sage, I don't know your daddy, man. But tell me about Olivia's daddy." I couldn't believe Dap was egging Sage on with this story about his little girlfriend, but I couldn't wait to hear what happened.

"Olivia isn't really my girlfriend. Her daddy told her she couldn't have a boyfriend until she's older. I'm not trying to hear what he's talking about though. That's why I need to know who my daddy is, so he can tell Oliva's daddy to let me be great. Oliva is my Queen and he's trying to keep her away from me."

I looked at Bria, and she hunched her shoulders. "What are you teaching this boy?" I asked, amused.

"Mommy can't teach me to be a man, but the dudes on YouTube know a little something. So, Uncle Donovan and Uncle

Wes, will y'all help me find my daddy?" Sage asked, looking back and forth between the two of us.

"That's something your mama will have to help you with. I don't know who the ni—the man is," I told him truthfully. "But to be honest, I agree with Olivia's daddy. If she is really your queen, she will be there when y'all get older."

"You sound just like Mommy!" Sage screeched.

"Well, she told you the right thing. Concentrate on school so you can be smart and go to college. Then you will be able to get a good job to take care of your queen," I explained to him. Sage had a frown on his face and I didn't want to see the little fella cry. "How about we go around the room and introduce you to the rest of your family. Would you like that?"

"Yes, I would. It's been just me and Mommy so I'm happy to have uncles and a grandpa." Sage smiled.

I stood up and pointed at Beverly. "That is your Grandma Bev. Go give her a hug."

Sage walked slowly towards my mama and stood in front of her. "You're beautiful like Olivia. Her skin is just like yours," he said, hugging her around the waist. "I've never had a grandma before."

"Well, you are handsome yourself, Sage. Guess what? I've never had a grandson before either," Beverly said, looking down at him.

"You have me now, Grandma Bev. Are you my mommy's mommy?" Sage asked.

Beverly looked over at Bria and smiled before turning her attention back to Sage. "Yes, I am," she beamed stooping down to his level.

Sage kissed her cheek and turned to the next person, which was my Pops. "I already met you in the car, Grandpa," he said cheerfully. He looked over at Tana and winked his eye and blew her a kiss. "I know you too, beautiful."

"Hold the fuck up, young'un. That's not ya girl. She belongs to me." Dap stalked over to Tana and wrapped his arms around her.

"You better keep her happy. I get an allowance you know." Sage smirked as he walked over to the couch Justice was sitting on.

This kid was too much for me. It was obvious that he was around Bria all the time because he was very advanced for a five-year-old. Maybe she should take away his online privileges, because he was learning a little too much of the wrong things. Sage watched as she fed Faith and I paid attention to the way Justice was staring at him in return. There was something in her eyes, but I couldn't pinpoint what it was. She looked down at Faith then back up at Sage and her eyebrows furrowed.

"Hi, I'm Sage. Is this your baby?" he asked Justice.

"Yes, this is your baby cousin Faith and I'm Justice." She smiled at Sage.

"She's pretty. Do Faith have a daddy?" he asked.

"As a matter of fact, she does. Your uncle Wes is her father."

"I hope I get a daddy soon. Faith is lucky," Sage said sadly.

"I'm quite sure your mommy will find your daddy really soon," Justice said, eyeing Bria.

Beverly clapped her hands together, getting everyone's attention. "We will finish this conversation later. Right now, it's time for us to eat, because I'm starving. I cooked some fried chicken, pinto beans, candied yams, and cornbread. Go wash up, now," she said loudly.

The tension in the room was thick enough to cut with a knife. I didn't know what was on Justice's mind, but I knew she was going to tell me later once we left my parents' house. I went to the bathroom down the hall to wash my hands and Dap came in behind me.

"What's up with Justice, brah?" he asked, leaning against the doorframe.

"I don't know. Maybe she's still mad from the baby shower. I know Bria did some foul shit, but what does that have to do with Sage?"

"She wasn't mean to nephew. It's just the way she looked at him, man. I truly think Justice has the same thoughts as me running through her head. Sage looks just like you, Wes."

"The only way Sage could be mine is if I slept with my sister. That shit never fuckin' happened, so both of y'all can get that shit outta here. I guess our genes skipped a generation or something and that's the reason he looks so much like me. I'm not with that incest shit at all. That's nasty as fuck!"

"I'm not implying that you slept with Bria, Wes. Calm the fuck down. I'm trying to figure out when she was ever pregnant. Something's fishy about this whole secret baby thing. It's not sitting well with me. On top of that, she can't even tell us who the fuck the father is. The nigga ain't even helping her take care of Sage," he said, walking to the sink to wash his hands.

"That's her business. If she wants us to know, she'll tell us eventually. I'm not about to hound her to tell us though. I'm about to go in there and eat some of this good ass food Mama stirred up in the kitchen."

I left Dap in the bathroom and slowly made my way down the hall. Everything Dap said made sense. Sage did look a lot like me, but I wasn't about to question the man upstairs about his creation.

Chapter 18
Beverly

It had been years since all three of the kids were in our home at the same time. The kitchen was chaotic because everyone was trying to pile their plates full of my good food. Bria was putting small portions on a plate for Sage and I started trying to pinpoint when she was ever pregnant. Nothing was coming to mind.

"Bev, what do you want to eat?" Wes Sr. asked.

"I little bit of everything, babe."

Walking to the table, Sage had his eyes glued to his tablet. I sat in my chair at the far end of the table and stared at him. He looked so much like Wes when he was little and I fell in love. We might have lost out on six years, but there was a lifetime of making up to do. Sage was so intelligent and very outspoken. I didn't expect anything less from a King's man.

Justice took a seat at the table across from Sage and after a while, everyone else joined us. Wes Sr. said a prayer and we sat quietly eating. The only sound heard was the clacking of silverware to the plates.

"Sage, how is your food?" I asked after swallowing the food in my mouth.

"It's good! I've never had food like this," he said, taking a sip of sweet tea. "Mommy, you have to learn to cook like Grandma Bev, this food is bangin'!"

Bria looked over at me and rolled her eyes. I didn't know why she was directing her anger at me, but I would let her attitude go on the strength of Sage. Wes Sr. must've seen Bria's reaction because he cleared his throat and dropped his fork into his plate.

"Bria, after we finish eating, I suggest you and Bev go into my office and have a conversation."

"I'm not ready to have that talk," she said, biting into a chicken wing.

"Let me rephrase that. You and Bev will have a conversation in my office after the table is cleared. Is that understood?" he sneered.

"There's nothing to talk about. I'm good on all that," Bria sassed.

"Well, I'm not, and you heard what I said. Don't make me go in on your ass in front of your son."

"Speaking of your son," Justice said, sitting back in her chair. "He looks so much like your brother, don't you think?"

Bria started fidgeting in her seat and a bead of sweat appeared on her top lip. She swiped it away, but kept her eyes on her plate. She was saved by the ringing of her phone and hopped up to answer it.

"Excuse me. I'll be right back; I have to answer this. Oh, and Justice, mind your business. Like Wes said earlier, he is my brother. You don't have anything to worry about. Faith is his only child and Sage is mine." Bria walked out of the room as she answered her phone.

Wes was staring at Justice as if he was about to get on her about what she said. Justice wasn't giving him any attention as she continued eating her food. She looked up, tilting her head to the side because Wes was still burning a hole in her face.

"Say what's on your mind, Wes." Justice sat up straight, ready for whatever.

"Why do you insist on bringing that up after we've already discussed the situation?"

"First of all, I don't give a damn about the bloodline. It's highly unlikely for a baby to look exactly like his uncle. There will be some type of resemblance, but being a spitting image, nah, I'm not buying that shit. I'll leave it alone for now. The truth will come out eventually."

Justice got up from the table, taking her plate into the kitchen. Sage was sitting with his tablet and headphones in his ear so he didn't witness any of the madness that was brewing between the adults. I took that opportunity to go find Bria, because the talk we needed to have was well overdue.

My husband told me about the conversation he and Bria had and I felt guilty for not telling her about Rita. He didn't think it was important for her to know I had taken on the responsibility of being her mother. Wes always wanted her to feel the love that I produced so there were no questions asked about biology.

When Bria moved away, we thought she just wanted to get out on her own. Hearing that she found out I wasn't her biological mother; I knew she had lost all respect for me regardless of how good of a mother I'd been her entire life. Bria felt betrayed and she had every right, but she had to take into consideration how much love was put behind the care I provided for her.

I walked into my room and retrieved the letters from the box in my closet before going out to find Bria. As I got closer to the staircase, I could hear Bria's low voice coming from the basement. Opening the door, I descended the stairs and found Bria sitting in a chair with her back turned away from me. The creak of the stairs caused her to turn around quickly and she immediately said her goodbyes to whomever was on the other end and hung up the phone.

"I'm not ready to talk to you, Beverly," she said, rolling her eyes.

"It's time for us to talk, Bria. It's been long overdue." I took a seat on the sofa in front of her and her eyes lowered to the envelopes I held in my hand. "I'm sorry I didn't tell you about your mother."

"You wouldn't be saying you're sorry if I hadn't found out. Why didn't you tell me? All my life you had me believing you were my mother!"

"You're right, I did take on the role of being your mother because it was part of what I signed up for when I forgave your father for his infidelities. The day we found out about you being left in the hospital alone, there were no questions asked. I just got up and went," I explained sincerely. "Bria, you were hooked up to so many machines. When the nurse told us there were traces of heroin in your system, I couldn't leave your side. I was with you every day, all night, for two months straight. There wasn't anyone on earth that could tell me you weren't my baby. I loved on you from day one."

"But you didn't tell me you weren't my biological mother!" Bria yelled at me. "I should've been told! Then I find out my mother died and y'all expect me to act like she never existed. I never got the chance to ask her why she left me!" Bria cried.

"That's the reason this talk is needed. Neither me nor your father hated Rita at all. Was it fucked up how she handled the situation? Yes, it was. But she kept in touch and we allowed her to visit anytime she wanted to see you. Our only stipulation for her was, she couldn't take you out of our home alone."

I looked down at the envelopes in my hand and knew I needed to give them to Bria. They had never been opened because they were addressed specifically to her, and Rita wanted Bria to read what was enclosed. It was hard for Wes not to open the letters, but I was there to make sure he didn't. The letters came often until they stopped suddenly and we found out Rita passed away.

"Here are all the letters Rita wrote for you for the first five years of your life. I'm quite sure all of your questions will be answered somewhere within those pages. Bria, I'm so sorry for being the best mother I could ever be to a child that I didn't actually birth." Rising to my feet, I stood over Bria while trying to see things from my point of view.

"Regardless of what you have said, I've never treated you any differently than I did Wes. Both of you received all my love. Bitterness set in once you found out the truth and you needed someone to blame. I'll take the heat, but I want you to know, I love you so much, Bria. Think about everything I've said and allow your mother to explain things further. Here are the letters. Read them, and hopefully you get the closure you're looking for."

Handing Bria the stack of envelopes, I kissed the top of her head and she shied away a little bit. I took that as my cue to leave her alone until she had read the letters. I truly didn't know if Rita's words would get her to see things from a different perspective, but I was prepared to pray that they would.

I climbed the stairs slowly and joined the rest of the family in the living room. *The Lego Movie 2* was playing on the TV and everyone was enjoying it with Sage except Wes and Justice. I made my way to the couch along the wall, taking the long route so I wouldn't block anyone's view of the television. As soon as I was seated, I looked over at my husband and he leaned over, planting a kiss on my cheek.

"Where's Wes and Justice?" I asked in a low tone.

"They went home."

When I was about to ask him another question, Bria appeared in the doorway. "Daddy, can I borrow your car?"

"Where are you going, Bria?"

"I just need to get out for a while. I won't be gone long. Would you keep an eye on Sage for me too?" she asked.

"Yes, he will be okay. Be careful out there, Bria. Take the Honda, not my BMW," he said sternly. "The keys are hanging on the wall hook by the door."

"Thank you," she said, giving Sage a kiss. "Be good, baby," Bria shot over her shoulder as she headed for the door.

Donovan got up and gave me a kiss and hugged his father. "We're going to head out as well. I've had a long day," he said, stretching. Tana rose from the loveseat and went to the closet to get her coat.

"Thank you for dinner, Bev. I will have to cook for you soon."

"I'll take you up on that, but you better not disappoint me. I don't eat everybody's cooking, so you have to come with it, girl."

"I got you," Tana replied with confidence. "You ready, baby?"

"Let's get out of here, beautiful. Pops, I'll call you soon because I have some things to fill you in on." Dap followed Tana to the door, and then there was three.

Sage was dozing off, but he wasn't quite asleep. I couldn't wait until it was just me and Wes, because I needed to express my thoughts on the day's events.

Chapter 19
Shanell

I had been calling Bria's ass all day and she kept sending me to voicemail. Usually when I hit her up, she would answer promptly, but after she left my apartment the day that I left Sage alone, Bria had been acting mighty funny. The last time I called her phone, she answered quickly. There were voices in the background, but I couldn't make out who they belonged to.

Bria had obviously gone somewhere quiet because there was no background noise when she got back on the phone with me. "What's up, Shanell?"

"Where are you, Bria? There's nobody in Michigan that you kick it with like that, so you have to be somewhere familiar."

"I'm at my father's house, since you're being nosy," she snapped. "What do you want?"

"Where is Sage?" I asked.

"He's upstairs. Would you please tell me what you want?"

"I haven't talked to you since the last time you were here. Bria, you've been ignoring me and I want to know why."

"You already know why I gave you space. How did you think I would stay in contact with you after you threatened to out me to my family? That shit was lame as fuck, Shanell. The shit you doing to Wes needs to stop. Just go on with your life. It's over between y'all."

"Bitch, where did all of this shit come from? You were all for helping me get back at your brother and now you want to fall back? Why now, Bria?" I yelled in her ear.

"Shanell, just leave it alone. I was mad at Wes for all the wrong reasons, and I should have never gone against him. Wes is truly happy with Justice and he deserves that shit. I'm out of it and you should be too, for real."

I sat back on my bed and wanted to slap her ass through the phone. Playing it cool was something I had to do so Bria would think I was on board with the bullshit she suggested. In all honesty, I was far from trying to move on without Wes being in my life.

"You're right. I've done enough damage in his life and I swear I'm done," I said after a long pause.

"Good. I think you should try to pursue something long term with Curt. He really has feelings for you, and there's no reason for the two of you to hide your relationship anymore. My brother wouldn't give a damn who you're dating nowadays."

Muting the phone, I laughed very hard because Bria didn't know about what happened to Curt. That nigga was maggot food, so he wouldn't be fucking on anyone ever again in life. Releasing one last chuckle, I unmuted the phone. I was about to lie to her for the second time, but she started talking before I could.

"I have to go. I'll talk to you later," she said, hanging up abruptly.

I glanced at the phone. I believed she didn't want anybody to know she was talking to me and ended the call. Bria wasn't about to get a chance to blow the whistle on me. There was a reason she was back in Chicago without informing me first. She would usually have me watch Sage, but since I left him alone in my apartment, she was holding that against me. Knowing she had Sage with her, she had to explain why she kept him a secret. Frantically unlocking my phone, I sent Bria a text message.

Me: Come to my house. I know you had to explain shit to your parents about Sage. I'm here for you, friend.

I waited for Bria to respond and when she didn't, I decided to take a nap. Loud knocking on my door jolted me out of my sleep. Looking around my semi-dark bedroom, I sat up in the bed to make sure there was actually someone knocking. A few seconds later, the knocking continued and I jumped up and raced to the front of my apartment.

Peeking through the peephole, I saw Bria standing on the other side. Unlocking the deadbolt lock, I pulled the door open and stepped to the side. She stepped inside and stopped next to the door without attempting to move from that spot. I closed the door and sat Indian style on the couch.

"You can have a seat." I motioned to the loveseat.

142

"I won't be here long. You wanted to know how things went with Sage meeting my family. Shanell, I have to tell them the truth. I don't know how long I can continue to lie," she said nervously.

"You will continue to tell the same story we came up with from the beginning. If you keep that story going, nobody can tell you it's not true. It's that simple."

"But it's not simple! They are speculating, especially Dap and Justice. I have to come clean about Wes being Sage's father. There's no getting around it. I survived the interrogation today, but I know it will come up again."

"Bria, you will keep your mouth closed! Wes would never forgive me if he knew I had that baby and told him his child died." I stalked over to her, getting in her face. We stood damn near nose to nose at that point.

"He's not going to forgive you for the recent shit you've done to him these past couple months either. Thinking about it, he's not going to forgive me either, but it's a chance I'm willing to take. Shanell, you didn't want Sage because Wes didn't want you. Yeah, he fucked you, but there was nothing else between y'all. You used the loss of the baby to manipulate him into taking care of you."

"He owed me for walking out of my life! I had to do whatever it took for him to be there for me. Don't cross this bridge, Bria. It won't end well for you, I promise," I said, pointing my finger in her face.

"There's nothing you can do to hurt me any more than the hurt I'm going to endure when my family finds out I hid the fact that my son is really my nephew. The truth will be told if you like it or not. This shit shouldn't have been done in the first place. For the past six years, I've betrayed my entire family. I won't do it a day longer."

Bria took a step back and I automatically wrapped my hands around her neck. Pushing her into the wall, I banged her head several times. She was gagging as she clawed at my hands, but I only pressed harder on her trachea. Bria's eyes rolled to the back of her head and I smirked wickedly. Her breathing became shallow and I had every intention to kill her so my secret would be safe.

Her head slumped to the side and I slowly loosened my grip on her neck. Bria started sliding down the wall and once I let her go, she landed on the floor with a thud. Bending down, I reached out to check for her pulse and her eyes popped open. Bria lifted her foot and kicked me hard in my pussy.

Doubling over, I dropped to my knees. Bria struggled to get up and stumbled to the door. Before she could get completely out, I crawled quickly and was able to grab her pants leg. She turned quickly and kicked me in the face and ran out of the apartment. I got up, snatched my keys from the table, and ran after her.

I was on her ass like white on rice as she fumbled to get the car keys out of her pocket. The keys fell to the ground, but she took off running down the street when realized she didn't have the keys, she turned to get them and saw me charging toward her. Jumping in my car, I hurried and backed out of the parking spot, never taking my eyes off Bria's silhouette as she ran away from my apartment. She cut into an alley and I smirked because I knew exactly what I planned to do. Gunning the car forward, I caught up with Bria in a matter of seconds.

She was running fast, but she had nothing on the engine that was in my Toyota Camry. I let down the window and yelled out to Bria as I slowed down a little bit. "Bria, stop and get in the car!"

"Fuck you, crazy bitch!" she screamed loudly without breaking her stride.

"That was the wrong thing to say," I laughed. "I gave you a chance to get in the car. Now you won't have to worry about anything else," I said so only I could hear.

Bria was almost to the end of the alley when I pushed my foot down on the gas. I started singing the *Nightmare on Elm Street* song that played when Freddy went after his victims in their sleep. My adrenaline was racing and I my love bud started beating rapidly. With the thought of killing, I was horny as fuck.

"One, two, Nelly's coming for you.
Three, four you shouldn't have knocked on my door.
Five, six, you're gonna feel real sick.

144

Seven, eight, you won't stay awake.
Nine, ten, you won't breathe again."

At that moment, I was doing about thirty miles per hour in the alley when I hit Bria from behind. Her body was lifted off the ground and onto the hood of my car. I didn't slow down and Bria ended up rolling off the car. When I looked in the rearview mirror, she was lying face down on the ground. She was motionless and I was satisfied with what I'd done. Before I rounded the corner, a man ran out of his yard to check on Bria.

I tore ass away from the scene and went back to my apartment. There was a dent in my hood, but I didn't care. Running up the stairs of my apartment building, I rushed into my apartment and packed a small bag before grabbing my phone and purse. Wasting no time at all, I was in and out of the apartment and on the road to find somewhere to sleep until I figured out where I would live. There was no way I could go back to my apartment after what I'd done to Bria.

Chapter 20
Wes

Faith was drooling on my face as I held her in the air over my head. She was smiling down at me while she laughed loudly. Justice had been very quiet since we got home from my parents' and I hadn't tried to figure out what her problem was. Instead, I'd been trying to tire Faith out so she could take her ass to sleep.

It was close to ten o'clock at night, I was getting sleepy and running out of ways to play with my daughter. Lying her on my chest, she rubbed her eyes vigorously and started whining. I pumped my fist because that was a sign that she was ready to call it a night. I patted Faith on the back and her eyes slowly closed as I started rocking back and forth. About fifteen minutes later, she was out like a light.

My phone vibrated on the nightstand and I couldn't get it without waking Faith. "Bae, would you answer my phone please?"

Justice got up and rushed to my side of the bed and grabbed my phone before it stopped ringing. "Hey, Ma," she said when she answered. She listened to what was being said then looked down at me with a concerned look on her face. "No, we haven't talked to anyone since we got home." Justice put her finger in her mouth and continued to listen. "Okay, I will let you know if she calls and you do the same, I don't care what time you call. Talk to you later. I'm sure she's fine."

She put the phone back on the nightstand and sat down on the edge of the bed. Justice ran her hand through Faith's hair and looked into my eyes. I could tell something was wrong but she hadn't said anything.

"What's going on, bae?" I asked.

"That was your mother. She said Bria left hours ago and she's not answering her phone. Both she and your father has been calling her phone repeatedly. When she comes back home, do she go missing for a long period of time?"

"Yeah, but if one of us calls her phone, she answers. Bria is not the type that would ignore my father at all. She knew he didn't play that shit. Here, take the baby and put her to bed," I said, removing my hand from Faith's back.

While Justice tended to Faith, I called my father to see what was going on. His phone went straight to voicemail when I called the first time, so I ended the call and tried again. He answered on the first ring.

"Wes, did she call you?" he asked quickly.

"No, what's going on?"

"Your sister left after talking to your mother and she said she just wanted to go out for a little while. That was hours ago and she hasn't answered her phone once. It rings until the voicemail picks up, but that's about all. I have a gut feeling something has happened to her."

"Where is Sage? Did she take him with her?" I asked.

"No, he's upstairs sleeping. Bria asked me if he could stay at the house with us and I told her yeah. Do me a favor and keep calling her phone. Maybe if she sees all of us calling, she will answer."

I remembered at one time my dad had Bria's phone connected to his Find My Phone app. "Pops, do you still have Bria's phone connected to the app to track her phone?"

"I didn't think about that! Thanks, son. Hold on a second." While he looked through the app, I stretched my arm out and grabbed the remote from Justice's side of the bed. Turning the channel on the phone, I surfed channels until *Boyz In the Hood* caught my attention.

"Wes, this thing has to be wrong. It's saying Bria's phone is at Cook County Hospital," Pops said slowly.

Hopping out of the bed, I scrambled around for a shirt. "It's usually pretty accurate, Pops. I'm about to make my way to the hospital. Meet me there. I will keep trying to call her phone." My voice shook with every word I spoke, I'd be the first to admit, I was scared.

"Okay. I'm getting ready to leave out now. Drive safely, son, and call your brother. See you soon," he said, hanging up.

I snatched a T-shirt from a hanger in the closet and threw it over my head. Justice entered the room and stopped abruptly as she watched me stuff my feet into my shoes. She stepped forward nervously, biting her lip.

"What's going on, Wes? Did y'all find Bria?"

"According to the tracker on her phone, she's at Cook County Hospital. I'm going to check it out with my Pops. Hopefully she is there for something minor. I'll call you when I find out," I said, kissing her on the lips as I rushed out of the bedroom.

Going through the kitchen I grabbed a banana and left out the door to the garage. As I got into my ride and turned the key in the ignition, my phone automatically connected to the Bluetooth. "Hey, Siri, call Dap," I said out loud as I backed out of the garage. The phone rang three times before his ass picked up.

"What up, brah? I'm in the middle of something," he said, breathing hard.

"You gon' have to get that nut another time. Meet me at Cook County Hospital."

"Cook County, for what?"

"Bria hasn't been answering her phone and Pops tracked it to the hospital. She's been gone for hours and nobody has heard from her," I explained.

"Shit, Bria left before me and Tana did. Yeah, that don't sound right, I'll be on my way in a minute."

"Aight, bro. Don't go back to fuckin'. This is not the time. This is some serious shit," I snapped.

"Nigga, fuck what you talking about! My lil nigga about to spit up before I go anywhere. You got me all the way fucked up," Dap said, hanging up.

My brother was something else, but I knew he wasn't leaving wet pussy for later.

I jumped on the expressway and pushed the gas, trying my best not to go over the speed limit too much. Thoughts of Bria filled my head and I silently prayed that she was alright. Regardless of the things she had done, she was still my sister and I would never want anything to happen to her.

Justice was all on my ass at my parents' house earlier. She kept talking about Sage and how he looked so much like me. I knew for a fact there was no way that boy was my son. Shit, the way I look at it, the lil nigga was going to have these hoes going crazy over him.

The inside of the car was too quiet, so I pushed the power button and went to the rap station on Sirius Radio. Eric B & Rakim's "I Ain't no Joke" was on and I rapped to that shit like I was performing it on stage. I loved old school rap and could listen to that shit all day.

"I ain't no joke I used to let the mic smoke
Now I slam it when I'm done and make sure it's broke
When I'm gone no one gets on 'cause I won't let
Nobody press up and mess up the scene I set
I like to stand in a crowd and watch the people wonder damn."

Rockin' to the beat, I cruised along the expressway, trying to keep a positive mindset as to why Bria was at the hospital. Song after song played and the music calmed me for the most part. My phone rang, interrupting my rap session. I glanced at the display and it was a private call. The first person that came to mind was Shanell and her bullshit. Declining the call, I kept driving until the phone rang once more.

"Yeah," was all I said when I answered.

"You miss me yet?" Shanell asked sweetly.

"I don't know what you on, but I'm not for your shit tonight, Shanell."

"All I did was asked a question. What crawled up your ass and died?"

"I told you not to contact me anymore! The shit you did was foul as fuck, and I hope you didn't think I wouldn't find out you drugged me at Mary's. The amount of Xanax you put in that drink wasn't necessary. Stay the fuck away from me and my family before I kill yo' crazy ass!"

"I see that white bitch ran her mouth, huh? Oh well, her day is coming. Anyway, when are you bringing that dick to me, Wes? I miss it," she chuckled.

"Fuck you, bitch! You will never get shit from me again!" I yelled.

"Wes, do you want to end up like Curt?" When she said that, I paused because I would've never thought Shanell would have been behind Curt's death. "Do I have your attention now? I saved your life that day, Wes. He was coming after you, and I couldn't let that happen."

"You didn't save me from shit! Try saving yourself, because you are going to meet your maker if you keep doing the shit you're doing. Commit yourself into somebody's facility, Shanell. Stop calling me!"

"Wes, you will be crying real soon, I promise. Enjoy the rest of your night, baby. I'll keep in touch."

Shanell hung up the phone and her words played repeatedly in my head. I couldn't figure out what she meant, but it didn't sit well with me. She was out of her mind, and I wished I had recorded the conversation to prove she killed that nigga Curt.

Signaling to get off the expressway at the Damen Avenue exit, I made a left and headed towards Polk Street to get to the hospital. I found a parking spot in the lot and grabbed my phone before getting out. As I walked into the emergency room entrance, my phone chimed with a text, but I ignored it, thinking it was Shanell. I made my way to the counter and waited behind a young lady that was talking to the employee on the other side. Looking down at my phone, I had a text from an unknown number. Opening the text, my heart dropped.

(773)555-8796: Hello, I am a nurse at Cook County Hospital. Your number was on the screensaver of a patient's phone that was brought in tonight. I need you guys, her family, to get to the hospital ASAP. Come through emergency and ask for Cheryl Lee. I'll explain in more detail when you get here.

When it was my turn to approach the counter, the employee behind it watched me walk up with a smile on his face. "Welcome to Cook County, how may I help you?"

"Yes, I received a message from a nurse saying one of my loved ones were here. Cheryl Lee is her name and she told me to mention her name when I arrived."

"Okay, let me find her number," he replied, tapping away on the keyboard. Once he found what he was looking for, he picked up the telephone and spoke lowly into the receiver. He kept avoiding my eyes as he listened then gently placed the receiver on the base. "Nurse Cheryl is on her way down. You can have a seat; she shouldn't be too long."

"Thank you," I said, walking away. I took a seat in an empty chair close to the counter. Taking my phone out, I dialed my Pops' number and waited for him to answer.

"Yeah, son. I'm walking in the hospital now. How far away are you?"

"I'm sitting in the waiting room of the emergency room. You'll see me when you come in," I saw my father coming through the automatic doors. Ending the call, I stood as he made his way toward me. Everyone in the room paused as he waltzed toward me. My Pops was still a good-looking nigga and he knew that shit.

"Is she here?" he asked, rubbing his hands together.

"Yeah, I believe she is. A nurse texted my phone as I was coming in and said she got my number off Bria's screensaver on her phone. I'm waiting on her to come down to tell me what the fuck is going on. Where did Bria say she was going when she left the house?"

"She didn't say. The only thing she asked was if she could use my ride, and I told her to take the Honda," he said as a dark-skinned nurse walked in our direction. She turned toward the guy behind the counter and he nodded his head, making her continue coming our way.

"Hello, I'm Cheryl Lee. I'm so glad I could get in contact of you. Follow me. I'll take you upstairs. We can discuss what's going on as we walk."

"First off, I would like to know the name of the person that you have upstairs. We want to make sure the person is our family member," Pops said.

"Well, according to the identification that was found in her purse, the patient is Bria King. Does that name ring a bell?"

"Yes, that's my daughter. Is she alright?" he asked.

"For the most part, yes. But she will need extensive rehabilitation," she said, leading the way to the elevators.

"What happened?" I asked as we entered the car when the doors opened.

"We don't know exactly what actually happened, but what I can tell you is that Bria is a very lucky young lady. According to the EMTs that brought her in, a Samaritan heard a woman scream out from his window. When he went into the alley behind his home, Bria was lying face down on the ground. A car rounded the corner before the guy could even see it. He only heard the engine roaring down the street," Nurse Cheryl explained as we neared the elevators and the doors opened.

"Bria had to have surgery. The femur bones in both legs were broken, her left ankle is fractured, and she has lacerations on her face," Nurse Cheryl said as the elevators opened on the fifth floor. "As I explained downstairs, Bria is going to go through an extensive rehabilitation. She is also going through emotional trauma, so we have her heavily sedated for pain and also to allow her to rest."

"Where did this happen?" Pops asked.

"The incident happened on Kilpatrick and Westend, right here on the west side," Cheryl said, stopping outside of room 525. "I will allow you guys to sit with her for a little bit, but visiting hours are over." She opened the door and Bria was lying on her back with both her legs raised by some type of machine.

"Why are her legs up like that?" I asked.

Cheryl stepped inside the room and closed the door behind her. "The machine is called a CPM machine. CPM stands for continuous passive machine. What the machine does is slowly move her joints because she can't do it on her own at this time. It prevents the joints from locking up and lose mobility. It also strengthens the muscles in her legs until she is ready for rehabilitation."

I walked around to the other side of the bed while my Pops stayed on the side closer to the door. Looking down at my sister, I saw the right side of her face was scarred pretty badly and it was going to take time to heal. She had small scratches all over her face and her lip was busted. Seeing her in the condition she was in pissed me off because someone lured her into that alley and I was mad because I couldn't kill the muthafucka responsible.

For the past couple months, the devil had been pushing me to the point of no return and for the moment, that nigga was winning. I was real close to saying fuck my career and going back to street mode full time.

Chapter 21
Dap

I never made it to the hospital because my ass was in a pussy coma after me and Tana sucked the soul out of each other. Of course, Wes and Pops called talking shit because Bria was indeed in the hospital. Wes was pissed because I didn't go running when he called. Hell, my dick was still in the pussy when I answered the fuckin' phone, so he was lucky he reached me when he did.

Hanging up on his ass was exactly what I did to prevent myself from saying something to him to hurt his sensitive ass feelings. I cuddled up under Tana and went back to sleep, but I felt bad because I didn't go to check on my little sister. When I was told she was sleeping and was alright for the most part, that eased my mind. There wasn't much I could do if the doctors weren't allowing us to stay up there with her.

It was seven in the morning and I was in the shower washing the sex residue off my body so I could head out to the hospital. Bria and I had our spats, but that didn't mean shit when one of us were hurt. I didn't agree with the way she handle the bullshit between Wes and Shanell but she was still my blood and I would be there any way I could. Actually, I was going to find out what the fuck happened and if I would have to kill the culprit.

Tana was still sleeping and I had no intentions of waking her. She needed that rest because I put my joint in her life and she was stuck. Stepping out of the shower, I grabbed a towel and dried off my body as I stared at myself in the mirror. It was time for me to get back into working out because my abs weren't as tight as they should've been.

Making a mental note to slide by the barbershop, I threw on my clothes after brushing my teeth. I stepped out of the bathroom and Tana was sprawled across my bed with half of her ass peeking from under the covers. My dick rocked up, but instead of acting on the thoughts in my head, I sat in the chair and threw on my all-black Nikes. I placed five one hundred-dollar bills on my pillow and wrote

Tana a quick note before grabbing my keys and phone from the dresser and made my way out the house.

When I got in my whip, I backed out of the driveway and headed straight for the hospital. Mentally getting my mind together to see my sister, I thought about all the things that had been going on in the King family. Finding out Beverly wasn't Bria's mother was a shock to both me and Wes. But being on the outside looking in, I would've never thought anything of that. Beverly had always treated us the same.

It took about thirty minutes for me to reach the hospital and that was because it was early and a Sunday morning. After finding a parking spot, I got out and walked into the building. After getting a pass, I got on the elevator and pushed the button for the fifth floor. As I walked down the hall and stopped outside of Bria's door, the sound of sniffling came from the other side and I quickly opened the door without knocking. Bria was lying on her back with tears running into her ears.

"Sis, you good?" I asked, walking further into the room. She shook her head no and I sat down in the chair beside the bed. "What do you need?"

"I'm hurting all over, Dap."

"Let me get a nurse in here so they can give you something for the pain," I said, rising from the chair.

"No!" she yelled. "The medicine makes me sleepy and I want to talk about what happened, but first, I want to tell you I'm sorry for anything I've ever said and done to you. Dap, we are family and believe it or not, I do love you."

"None of that matters right now, Bria. Tell me how you ended up lying in this bed. Start from the beginning."

"When I left the house last night, I went to see Shanell—"

"What the fuck did you need to see that crazy bitch for?" I asked heatedly.

"There's so much y'all don't know," she wept. "The whole family is going to be mad at me, Dap."

The door opened as I was about to respond and my Pops and Wes walked in with flowers and balloons. Bria started crying harder

156

and Pops rushed to her side grabbing her hand. Wes glanced at me like I was the reason she was bawling her eyes out.

"Talk to me, baby," Pops said, rubbing his finger back and forth over the top of her hand after placing the balloons on the nearest table. Wes did the same with the flowers.

"I fucked up!" she cried.

"What happened, Bria?" Wes asked. "What did you do, sis?"

"Like I was telling Dap, I went to visit Shanell—"

"Why the fuck would you meet up with her?" Wes snapped, cutting her off.

"If y'all would let me talk and stop interrupting me, then I can finish telling the story." Bria went from crying to getting mad and she had a point. We needed to hear what she had to say.

"Okay, we're listening," I said, sitting back in the chair. Pops sat on the side of the bed and Wes stood with his arms folded over his chest.

Bria stared at Wes and a lonely tear cascaded down her face. "Wes, I'm so sorry for siding with Shanell through all she has put you through. I hope you don't hate me," she choked out. "I went to see Shanell because the moment Sage and I entered our parents' home, there were speculations thrown at me about him looking like Wes."

My left eyebrow rose to the ceiling because I had a feeling some bullshit was about to come out of Bria's mouth. Instead of speaking prematurely, I sat waiting for the ball to drop. Wes hadn't put two and two together and stood waiting for the rest of the story. Me and Pops was on the same page because his lips tightened in a straight line, so I knew he grasped the small concept of the little bit of information that was given.

"I went to Shanell's apartment and tried to talk her into leaving you and Justice alone, Wes. She refused and threatened me. Let me go back to why I left Chicago and moved to Michigan. When I found out about my birth mother, I got upset and just wanted to get away from Beverly. I had planned the move a few months prior to Wes getting out of prison and had already secured an apartment."

Bria's voice was shaky as hell, but she fought through by taking a deep breath.

"Shanell came to my apartment after Wes found out she was messing around with Curt. She was saying how sorry she was for not holding you down while you were locked up. At that point, you hadn't been gone long at all, maybe a couple weeks. Shanell started experiencing pain in her stomach and I took her to the hospital. When I was able to go into the room, Shanell explained that she was experiencing a miscarriage and didn't want me to witness it. She told me to go home and she would call me."

Placing her arm over her face, Bria cried for the loss of her niece or nephew. "I didn't hesitate telling any of you what happened. What I didn't tell was the fact that Shanell had the baby," she sobbed loudly.

"What the fuck you mean she had the baby?" Wes yelled. "Where the fuck is my seed, Bria?"

"She put the baby up for adoption, Wes! When you told Shanell you were done with her, she gave the baby up because you didn't want to be with her! I went through hell and high water to track down that baby," she said as the tears continued to flow. "I did what I thought was right, for my family. Shanell found out somehow that I gained custody of the baby and told me to make sure nobody found out or I'd regret it. I had to keep the secret."

"Wait, are you trying to say that you had my seed in your custody all this time and didn't tell me?" Wes snarled. "Sage is *my* son, Bria?"

"Yes, Sage is your son. I'm so sorry Wes. I wanted to tell you; I swear."

Wes paced the floor and I could've sworn I saw smoke coming from his nostrils like a raging bull. "I just introduced myself to my son as his muthafuckin' uncle! He is damn near six years old and calls my sister his mother! Do he even know about Shanell?"

"He knows her as Auntie Nell. Wes, I didn't want to keep this from you. I had to. Shanell held this shit over my head for so many years and I didn't know how to get away from her. Introducing Sage to all of y'all told me I had to reveal the truth. Shanell didn't agree with me telling, so she tried to choke me to death. I got away from her and ran out of her apartment." Bria started breathing heavily, but continued to talk.

"My clumsy ass dropped the keys to the car, but I couldn't get them because Shanell was charging towards me. I took off running down the street and ducked off into an alley. Shanell chased me in her car and hit me from behind and left me for dead in the middle of a dirty ass alley. I'm lucky to be alive right now, but I brought this on myself."

"This is not your fault, baby. You did the right thing by going after Sage. Where you went wrong was when you kept this from us for so long. You should've come to me and I could've helped," Pops said to Bria.

"I knew something was up when I laid eyes on Sage. I just didn't think Shanell was his mother. Wes, to be honest, I thought you were the reason Bria left because you slept with her," I said truthfully.

"What the fuck! I told yo' ass I wouldn't do no sick shit like that!"

"Look, bro, see this shit from my perspective. Bria was helping this bitch get back at you. She comes home with a whole baby that looks identical to your ass. If the tables were turned and Sage looked like me, what the fuck would you think?" I asked. When he didn't respond, I knew I had his ass thinking. "Exactly, nigga. So don't think I'm an asshole for thinking the way I did. Plus, I voiced that shit to you last night."

"Where the fuck does Shanell live?" Pops asked Bria.

"4951 West Westend Avenue, first floor. I don't think you will find her there. Shanell isn't dumb enough to stay after what she did. Then again, she may think I'm dead," Bria said, shaking her head.

Wes snatched the door open and I jumped up to follow him. "Dap, kill that bitch if she's there. I know that's where he's headed," Pops said before I could leave out the door.

By the time I got to the elevator, Wes was already on his way down to the lobby. Looking around, I spotted the stairway sign and ran for it. Jogging down the stairs as fast as I could, I finally got to the lobby floor and out the main entrance. Wes was peeling out of the parking lot at top speed and I had to catch up with him.

Hopping in my whip, I backed out without looking and damn near smacked a raggedy ass Cutlass. Slamming on my brakes, the stupid muthafucka kept creeping along the back of my car and stopped once he had me boxed in. I blew my horn but he acted like he didn't hear the shit. Throwing my car in park, I jumped out with my pistol in hand. It wasn't the time for the simple-minded shit the punk was on.

"What the fuck is your problem, nigga? Move your fuckin' car!" I snarled at his ass.

"CVL, nigga!" he yelled throwing up a gang sign.

I laughed in his face and raised my tool. "I'm not with that gang-bangin' shit, but I'll blow yo' muthafuckin' head off today! Whoever the fuck is guiding you niggas is doing that shit backwards. You got one chance to move this piece of shit or you're gon' be carried out of this bitch with a sheet over your ass."

"Damn, fool, it ain't that serious. I'm moving," he said, looking me up and down.

"Move, muthafucka!"

I had to jump back because his ass almost ran over my feet getting out of dodge. I tucked my bitch and got back in my car and sped out of the parking lot. Wes was nowhere in sight, but I knew my way through the city quite well. Knowing Wes, he didn't think before he drove off and took the street. I was about to eat up the expressway on his ass and beat him to Shanell's crib.

Taking the exit at Kostner on I-290, I made a right turn onto Kostner and cruised to Madison Street. When I made the left turn down Madison, I beelined toward Cicero and saw Wes's car just ahead of me. "What the hell this nigga do, fly to this muthafucka?" I asked myself as I watched him bend the corner.

I pulled up to the intersection and glanced to my left to see if there were any cars coming. When the coast was clear, I turned down Cicero and hit Westend Avenue. When I hit Shanell's block, Wes was already stomping down the street. There was an empty spot directly across the street from the building Wes had entered. I pulled in and snatched the keys from the ignition and ran inside.

Wes had kicked Shanell's door in and was stalking through the house looking for her devious ass. Of course, she wasn't there. Walking into one of the rooms behind him, he started rustling through papers on her dresser.

"Brah, she ain't here. Let's go before somebody calls twelve. You done kicked this hoe's door in and everything," I said from the doorway.

"I'm gon' kill this bitch! She's been lying for years and used the one thing I felt bad about against me! Then she hit my sister with a muthafuckin' car! She could've killed her, man. I have to find this crazy bitch before she attacks again. This was the last fuckin' straw and she gon' pay," Wes said, leaving the bedroom in a huff.

As we walked toward the front door, a woman appeared in the doorway. "Y'all looking for Shanell?" she whispered.

"Yeah, you know where she's at?" Wes asked.

"Nah, she was in here fighting with a female last night, but I don't know what happened. All I know is a few minutes after they ran out of the building, Shanell came back and left with a bag as quickly as she came," she said, looking over her shoulder. "Something's not right with that chick. She seems very dangerous. I found these keys outside. I don't know if they mean anything, but here."

Taking the keys from her hand, I looked down at them and sure enough, they were the keys to Pops' Honda. "If she shows back up, hit my line," I said, pulling one of my business cards out of my wallet. "Use that number only if you see Shanell. My woman don't play that bullshit and there won't be nothing I'll be able do if she taps that ass. I'm not talking in a good way either."

"I got a man. There's no reason for me to call you because you're not even my type," the female said, rolling her eyes.

Ignoring her because she was a little upset and it showed, I led the way out of the building with Wes on my heels.

"Brah, where are you about to go?" I asked Wes.

Chapter 22
Beverly

"Miss Beverly, where's my mommy?" Sage asked from the doorway of the kitchen.

I looked up from the newspaper I was reading and the poor baby had tears in his eyes. Bria took very good care of Sage and it showed. My husband left very early to go back to the hospital to sit with Bria and neither one of us wanted to tell Sage that she was hurt. I didn't want to lie to him, but I couldn't tell him the truth either.

"She will be back soon, baby, and I want you to call me Grandma or Grandma Bev, okay?" Sage nodded his head yes and the tears flowed down his cheeks. "Come here," I said, pulling out one of the chairs taking a seat. Sage slowly walked toward me and stood next to the table. "Has it only been you and your mama back home?" I asked, hugging him close to my chest.

Sage shook his head again and I wasn't going to let that gesture slide a second time. "Open your mouth and talk. You showed me last night that's something you love to do. Big boys speak their minds, not shake their heads."

"Yes, it's me and Mommy all the time. Auntie Nell calls me a lot on video, but that's about it. I wish I had a daddy though," he said sadly, stepping out of my embrace.

Hearing him reference Shanell made me cringe. So many scenarios were playing in my mind and the puzzle pieces were starting to fit in place. Shanell knew about Sage, but no one in this family knew a thing except Bria. Sage is Wes' son; my intuition was never wrong, and I knew I was right. Concentrating on Sage at the moment was my only concern. The other shit would get handled accordingly.

"It's not the end of the world if you don't have a daddy. You have Uncle Wes and Uncle Donovan. They can do all things your daddy would do if he was around. Are you willing to give them a chance?"

"I like my new uncles; they're cool and funny. I can't wait to spend time with them." Sage smiled, but it didn't last long. He dropped his head and his shoulders drooped as he spoke again. "Miss Bev—I mean Grandma Bev, why my daddy don't want to be around me? Did I do something to make him not love me?"

For Sage to be five years old, he was a very observant little boy. He was wise beyond his years and there was no telling how many questions he had bottled up waiting for answers.

"I don't think your daddy doesn't want to be around you, baby. Why he isn't around is something I don't have the answer to. But one day I hope you get the chance to ask your father those questions. I want you to know this, there is nothing you have done to make your daddy not love you. As long as your mommy loves you, that's all that should matter right now. I love you too, you know."

"How do you love me and you just met me?" Sage asked as he pulled out the chair next to him and sat down.

"The love I have for you is automatic because you are my family. A grandma knows her babies even when she just met them." I winked at him. "Now what do you want to eat for breakfast?" I asked, standing to my feet.

"Cocoa Pebbles!" Sage said, clapping his hands.

"Yeah, your mommy got you hooked on that cereal, huh?" I laughed. "When I found out she was coming home, I went out and bought a box just for her."

"Mommy doesn't eat my kind of cereal. She says it's too sweet, but that's good because there's more for me!" he exclaimed, throwing his hands in the air.

As I prepared a bowl of cereal for Sage, a thought came to mind. Placing the bowl in front of him, I picked up my cell phone from the counter and dialed my next door neighbor Clara. It was a little after ten so I knew she was awake having her third cup of coffee.

"Good morning, Bev," she said cheerfully. "You had quite a gathering last night. What was the occasion?"

"Girl, it wasn't a gathering. All the kids were just over at the same time. They are all grown up and the family is getting bigger as the years goes by," I said proudly.

"I already know how that goes. I've been a grandma for quite some time and I'm tired, shit," Clara laughed. "This is just the beginning for you. Get all the kisses you can, because they grow up so fast."

"Oh, I plan on doing just that. I have a question. Did Priscilla and the boys come over this weekend?"

"More like Priscilla dropped them off and left," Clara huffed. "Why do you ask?"

"Well, Bria came home and she has a son." I paused.

"Lil Bria had a baby! Congratulations, Bev." I could hear Clara stomping her feet with excitement, and I couldn't stop myself from laughing. "How old is the baby?"

"Almost six," I said, knowing she was going to be just as surprised as I was when I found out.

"Six? That's the same age as the twins! Where the hell was the baby when she came home all those times through the years?"

"I don't know, but I will have some answers when Wes Sr. comes home. That's a conversation for another day. I was wondering if Sage could come over to play with the twins in your yard. He is an advanced one and I wanted him to have some fun with kids his own age."

"That's no problem. Those knuckle heads are out there right now, as a matter of fact. So bring him over whenever you're ready." Clara said.

"Okay, let me get him dressed and I'll see you in a few. Thanks, Clara."

"Beverly King, get off my phone," she said, hanging up on me.

Sage was drinking the milk from his bowl. When he lowered it, there was milk falling from his chin. He looked up at me with a wicked grin on his face. Wes used to do the same thing when he was Sage's age, and it took me back in time.

"Come on, greedy. We're going next door so you can meet Lonnie and Ronnie. They are good boys and they are the same age as you. Would you like that?" I asked.

"Yes! I miss my friends back home, but I love meeting new people. I just hope they are not bullies, because I don't play well with those kinds of people."

"Nah, they won't bully you, baby. If they do, I'm quite sure you won't let them get away with it. Tell Miss Clara and she will set them straight, then you can ask her to call me and I will come get you, alright?"

"Okay, Grandma Bev. I'm gonna go take a shower and change my clothes. I'll be ready in a little bit," he said hopping out of the chair.

I could hear his little feet stomping up the stairs and I just smiled because he reminded me so much of Wes it wasn't funny. Cleaning up Sage's mess, I rinsed the bowl and spoon before putting both in the dishwasher. I picked up my phone to call my husband to get word on Bria, but a sound at the back door got my attention. Peeking out the window, I looked around the yard, but saw nothing out of the norm.

Ignoring the uneasy feeling running through my body, I turned from the window and wiped down the table. Ten minutes had passed as I climbed the stairs to check on Sage. He was in Bria's old room tying his shoes when I walked in. I'd never seen a little kid dress himself like a grown man. Wes always needed help.

Sage had picked out a blue #Iamtheghostwriter hoodie, a pair of dark blue jeans, and a pair of blue high-top Converse sneakers. He had brushed his hair and washed his face as well. The kid looked good to me and he was ready to go out and play.

"I'm ready, Grandma Bev. How do I look?" he asked, posing with his hand under his chin.

"You look like you belong on the front of a magazine. Let's go play," I said, grabbing his hand as we went down the stair.

***

I sat and talked to Clara for a few before I left Sage in her care to clean up a little bit back at the house. Sage assured me he would be fine since he and the twins hit it off really good. I left them in the backyard throwing a football as they warmed up for a game. The twins invited more of their friends to come over to meet Sage and play.

Walking back to my house, I had decided to go through my backyard since the twins were already out there. As I climbed the stairs and opened the door, there was a sweet smell of perfume that wasn't there when I left. Creeping inside slowly, I left the door opened just in case I needed to run back outside. I flipped the light switch on the wall as I walked through the kitchen and eased toward the living room.

When I entered the room, there was someone sitting on my sofa with her back facing the kitchen. I had no clue who had took the liberty of entering my home without my permission, but I hoped they were ready for a fight. The person was looking straight ahead and knew I was behind them.

"Hello, Beverly," the intruder greeted me as she stood up and turned around.

"Shanell, what the fuck are you doing in my house?"

"With all the shit going on, you should never leave your doors unlocked, *Mother*," she cackled loudly. "To answer your question, I came to get my son," she smirked.

My revelations were correct all alone and Sage being Wes's son was confirmed. Shanell was not about to make it easy for us to get to know Sage. She wanted Wes to forever think his child was dead.

"You don't have a son, Shanell," I said, trying play along like I had no idea what she was talking about. "Shanell, you lost your child. Are you okay, baby?"

"Cut the bullshit, Beverly! Where the fuck is Sage?" she screamed.

I looked around the room, trying to find something in close proximity to knock her ass out with if need be. Shanell walked around the sofa toward me and I backed up slowly. She had a look of pure evil in her eyes and I'd never seen her that way before.

"Aht, aht, where you going?" she asked, grabbing me by the front of my shirt.

I punched her ass in the face, causing her to let me go briefly. Next thing I knew, she came out of her pocket with what looked like a box cutter. My eyes widened and I turned to run to the guest room to get away from her, but she caught up with me. Putting her arm around my neck from behind, Shanell held the blade to the side of my face.

"Shanell, don't do this," I said without fear. I was ready for whatever and if I had to die, I was going out fighting.

"Where. The. Fuck. Is. My. Son!" she screamed, digging the blade into my cheek.

"Why didn't you tell us you had the baby, Shanell? We would've been there for you."

"Y'all don't give a damn about me! Bria didn't even give a fuck about me, and that's why the bitch is lying in the morgue now. Fuck all of y'all! I told Wes he was going to cry, and I meant that shit." She laughed. "See, if he hadn't played with my feelings, you wouldn't be in this position, Beverly. You can thank your son for your death, because he wanted to play with a bitch off her meds."

"Shanell, you are a bright young lady and have a wonderful future ahead of you—"

"Shut the fuck up, bitch! My future is shot and you know it. I killed Curt, I killed Bria, and I'm about to kill your ass too, as soon as you tell me where my son is. I am going to leave with my baby and disappear."

If she thought she was taking that boy anywhere, she was out of her fucking mind. I said a silent prayer before I lowered my chin to my chest and reeled my head back with all my might. The grip Shanell had on neck loosened and I turned around and kicked her ass in the stomach. She doubled over and I hit her with a lamp that I grabbed from the end table.

Shanell fell on the floor and I stood over her. She wasn't dead, but she was out cold. Racing to the kitchen I grabbed my phone and dialed 911.

"911 what is your emergency?"

"Yes, I have an intruder in my house and I need the police here quickly," I said into the phone. Shanell was still on the floor as I talked to the operator. "The address is 2900 Lynwood Court in Flossmoor, please hurry."

"Ma'am, stay on the line, I have a few more questions," the operator said.

"Fuck the questions! This bitch is still in my house," I yelled into the phone, turning my back briefly, but when I turned back around, Shanell was snarling in my face with blood dripping from her nose.

Grabbing me by my shirt, she punched me in the face and I dropped the phone. The operator was saying something, but I couldn't make out her words. Before I knew what was happening, Shanell raised the box cutter and slid it across my throat. My hand immediately wrapped around the open wound. I was hoping I could stop the bleeding, but I knew it was impossible.

I dropped to my knees and she plunged the blade into my chest repeatedly. I fell over on my side and knew I wouldn't live to save my family from this bitch.

To Be Continued...
Paid in Karma 3
Coming Soon

Submission Guideline

Submit the first three chapters of your completed manuscript to ldpsubmissions@gmail.com, subject line: Your book's title. The manuscript must be in a .doc file and sent as an attachment. Document should be in Times New Roman, double spaced and in size 12 font. Also, provide your synopsis and full contact information. If sending multiple submissions, they must each be in a separate email.

Have a story but no way to send it electronically? You can still submit to LDP/Ca$h Presents. Send in the first three chapters, written or typed, of your completed manuscript to:

LDP: Submissions Dept
Po Box 870494
Mesquite, Tx 75187

DO NOT send original manuscript. Must be a duplicate.

Provide your synopsis and a cover letter containing your full contact information.

Thanks for considering LDP and Ca$h Presents.

BOW DOWN TO MY GANGSTA

By **Ca$h**

TORN BETWEEN TWO

By **Coffee**

THE STREETS STAINED MY SOUL **II**

By **Marcellus Allen**

BLOOD OF A BOSS **VI**

SHADOWS OF THE GAME II

By **Askari**

LOYAL TO THE GAME **IV**

By **T.J. & Jelissa**

A DOPEBOY'S PRAYER **II**

By **Eddie "Wolf" Lee**

IF LOVING YOU IS WRONG… **III**

By **Jelissa**

TRUE SAVAGE **VII**

MIDNIGHT CARTEL III

DOPE BOY MAGIC III

By **Chris Green**

BLAST FOR ME **III**

A SAVAGE DOPEBOY III

CUTTHROAT MAFIA II

By **Ghost**

A HUSTLER'S DECEIT III

KILL ZONE **II**

BAE BELONGS TO ME III

By **Aryanna**

Meesha

THE COST OF LOYALTY **III**
By **Kweli**
CHAINED TO THE STREETS II
By **J-Blunt**
KING OF NEW YORK V
COKE KINGS IV
BORN HEARTLESS IV
By **T.J. Edwards**
GORILLAZ IN THE BAY V
TEARS OF A GANGSTA II
De'Kari
THE STREETS ARE CALLING II
Duquie Wilson
KINGPIN KILLAZ IV
STREET KINGS III
PAID IN BLOOD III
CARTEL KILLAZ IV
Hood Rich
SINS OF A HUSTLA II
ASAD
TRIGGADALE III
Elijah R. Freeman
KINGZ OF THE GAME V
Playa Ray
SLAUGHTER GANG IV
RUTHLESS HEART III
By **Willie Slaughter**
THE HEART OF A SAVAGE III
By **Jibril Williams**
FUK SHYT II

172

Paid in Karma 2

By Blakk Diamond
THE DOPEMAN'S BODYGAURD II
By Tranay Adams
TRAP GOD II
By Troublesome
YAYO III
A SHOOTER'S AMBITION II
By S. Allen
GHOST MOB
Stilloan Robinson
KINGPIN DREAMS II
By Paper Boi Rari
CREAM
By Yolanda Moore
SON OF A DOPE FIEND II
By Renta
FOREVER GANGSTA II
By Adrian Dulan
LOYALTY AIN'T PROMISED II
By Keith Williams
THE PRICE YOU PAY FOR LOVE II
By Destiny Skai
THE LIFE OF A HOOD STAR
By Rashia Wilson
TOE TAGZ III
By Ah'Million
CONFESSIONS OF A GANGSTA II
By Nicholas Lock
PAID IN KARMA III
By **Meesha**

173

Meesha

I'M NOTHING WITHOUT HIS LOVE II
By Monet Dragun
CAUGHT UP IN THE LIFE II
By Robert Baptiste
NEW TO THE GAME II
By **Malik D. Rice**
Life of a Savage II
By **Romell Tukes**
Quiet Money II
By **Trai'Quan**

Available Now

RESTRAINING ORDER **I & II**
By **CA$H & Coffee**
LOVE KNOWS NO BOUNDARIES **I II & III**
By **Coffee**
RAISED AS A GOON I, II, III & IV
BRED BY THE SLUMS I, II, III
BLAST FOR ME I & II
ROTTEN TO THE CORE I II III
A BRONX TALE I, II, III
DUFFEL BAG CARTEL I II III IV
HEARTLESS GOON I II III IV
A SAVAGE DOPEBOY I II
HEARTLESS GOON I II III
DRUG LORDS I II III
CUTTHROAT MAFIA
By **Ghost**

LAY IT DOWN **I & II**

LAST OF A DYING BREED

BLOOD STAINS OF A SHOTTA I & II III

By **Jamaica**

LOYAL TO THE GAME I II III

LIFE OF SIN I, II III

By **TJ & Jelissa**

BLOODY COMMAS I & II

SKI MASK CARTEL I II & III

KING OF NEW YORK I II,III IV

RISE TO POWER I II III

COKE KINGS I II III

BORN HEARTLESS I II III

By **T.J. Edwards**

IF LOVING HIM IS WRONG…I & II

LOVE ME EVEN WHEN IT HURTS I II III

By **Jelissa**

WHEN THE STREETS CLAP BACK I & II III

THE HEART OF A SAVAGE I II

By **Jibril Williams**

A DISTINGUISHED THUG STOLE MY HEART I II & III

LOVE SHOULDN'T HURT I II III IV

RENEGADE BOYS I II III IV

PAID IN KARMA I II

By **Meesha**

A GANGSTER'S CODE I &, II III

A GANGSTER'S SYN I II III

THE SAVAGE LIFE I II III

CHAINED TO THE STREETS

By **J-Blunt**

Meesha

PUSH IT TO THE LIMIT
By **Bre' Hayes**
BLOOD OF A BOSS **I, II, III, IV, V**
SHADOWS OF THE GAME
By **Askari**
THE STREETS BLEED MURDER **I, II & III**
THE HEART OF A GANGSTA I II& III
By **Jerry Jackson**
CUM FOR ME I II III IV V
An **LDP Erotica Collaboration**
BRIDE OF A HUSTLA **I II & II**
THE FETTI GIRLS **I, II& III**
CORRUPTED BY A GANGSTA I, II III, IV
BLINDED BY HIS LOVE
THE PRICE YOU PAY FOR LOVE
By **Destiny Skai**
WHEN A GOOD GIRL GOES BAD
By **Adrienne**
THE COST OF LOYALTY I II
By Kweli
A GANGSTER'S REVENGE **I II III & IV**
THE BOSS MAN'S DAUGHTERS I II III IV V
A SAVAGE LOVE **I & II**
BAE BELONGS TO ME I II
A HUSTLER'S DECEIT I, II, III
WHAT BAD BITCHES DO I, II, III
SOUL OF A MONSTER I II III
KILL ZONE
By **Aryanna**
A KINGPIN'S AMBITON

A KINGPIN'S AMBITION **II**

I MURDER FOR THE DOUGH

By **Ambitious**

TRUE SAVAGE I II III IV V VI

DOPE BOY MAGIC I, II

MIDNIGHT CARTEL I II

By **Chris Green**

A DOPEBOY'S PRAYER

By **Eddie "Wolf" Lee**

THE KING CARTEL **I, II & III**

By **Frank Gresham**

THESE NIGGAS AIN'T LOYAL **I, II & III**

By **Nikki Tee**

GANGSTA SHYT **I II &III**

By **CATO**

THE ULTIMATE BETRAYAL

By **Phoenix**

BOSS'N UP **I , II & III**

By **Royal Nicole**

I LOVE YOU TO DEATH

By Destiny J

I RIDE FOR MY HITTA

I STILL RIDE FOR MY HITTA

By **Misty Holt**

LOVE & CHASIN' PAPER

By **Qay Crockett**

TO DIE IN VAIN

SINS OF A HUSTLA

By **ASAD**

BROOKLYN HUSTLAZ

Meesha

By **Boogsy Morina**

BROOKLYN ON LOCK I & II

By **Sonovia**

GANGSTA CITY

By **Teddy Duke**

A DRUG KING AND HIS DIAMOND I & II III

A DOPEMAN'S RICHES

HER MAN, MINE'S TOO I, II

CASH MONEY HO'S

By Nicole Goosby

TRAPHOUSE KING **I II & III**

KINGPIN KILLAZ I II III

STREET KINGS I II

PAID IN BLOOD **I II**

CARTEL KILLAZ I II III

By **Hood Rich**

LIPSTICK KILLAH **I, II, III**

CRIME OF PASSION I II & III

By **Mimi**

STEADY MOBBN' **I, II, III**

THE STREETS STAINED MY SOUL

By **Marcellus Allen**

WHO SHOT YA **I, II, III**

SON OF A DOPE FIEND

Renta

GORILLAZ IN THE BAY **I II III IV**

TEARS OF A GANGSTA

DE'KARI

TRIGGADALE I II

Elijah R. Freeman

178

GOD BLESS THE TRAPPERS I, II, III

THESE SCANDALOUS STREETS I, II, III

FEAR MY GANGSTA I, II, III

THESE STREETS DON'T LOVE NOBODY I, II

BURY ME A G I, II, III, IV, V

A GANGSTA'S EMPIRE I, II, III, IV

THE DOPEMAN'S BODYGAURD

Tranay Adams

THE STREETS ARE CALLING

Duquie Wilson

MARRIED TO A BOSS... I II III

By Destiny Skai & Chris Green

KINGZ OF THE GAME I II III IV

Playa Ray

SLAUGHTER GANG I II III

RUTHLESS HEART I II

By Willie Slaughter

FUK SHYT

By Blakk Diamond

DON'T F#CK WITH MY HEART I II

By Linnea

ADDICTED TO THE DRAMA I II III

By Jamila

YAYO I II

A SHOOTER'S AMBITION

By S. Allen

TRAP GOD

By Troublesome

FOREVER GANGSTA

By Adrian Dulan

Meesha

TOE TAGZ I II
By Ah'Million
KINGPIN DREAMS
By Paper Boi Rari
CONFESSIONS OF A GANGSTA
By Nicholas Lock
I'M NOTHING WITHOUT HIS LOVE
By Monet Dragun
CAUGHT UP IN THE LIFE
By Robert Baptiste
NEW TO THE GAME
By **Malik D. Rice**
Life of a Savage
By **Romell Tukes**
LOYALTY AIN'T PROMISED
By Keith Williams
Quiet Money
By **Trai'Quan**

Paid in Karma 2

BOOKS BY LDP'S CEO, CA$H

TRUST IN NO MAN
TRUST IN NO MAN 2
TRUST IN NO MAN 3
BONDED BY BLOOD
SHORTY GOT A THUG
THUGS CRY
THUGS CRY 2
THUGS CRY 3
TRUST NO BITCH
TRUST NO BITCH 2
TRUST NO BITCH 3
TIL MY CASKET DROPS
RESTRAINING ORDER
RESTRAINING ORDER 2
IN LOVE WITH A CONVICT

Coming Soon
BONDED BY BLOOD 2
BOW DOWN TO MY GANGSTA

CPSIA information can be obtained
at www.ICGtesting.com
Printed in the USA
LVHW022150170720
661013LV00010B/726

9 781951 081881